Thing
with
Feathers

Thing
with
Feathers
A Different Romance

Jonathan Pearce

http://www.balona.com

tive

C   and

Thing with Feathers
A Different Romance

First printing, 2001
Second printing, revised, 2003

Library of Congress Cataloging-in-Publication Data

Pearce, Jonathan.
  Thing with feathers: a different romance / by Jonathan Pearce.
     p. cm.
  ISBN 1-59411-012-3 (alk. paper)
  1. Vietnamese Conflict, 1961-1975--Veterans--Fiction.
  2. Loss (Psychology)--Fiction. 3. Marines--Fiction. I. Title.
  PS3616.E245T47 2003
  813'.6--dc21

                                        2003009653

The text of this book is set in Bookman Old Style
Cover design by Book Cover Express
Printed in the United States of America

Published by
The Writers' Collective
Cranston, Rhode Island

In memory of
Thomas Lyle Pearce
Semper Fi

Chapter One

His face is nearly unlined, even as it maintains its present strain. The old saw flashes through my mind that *at fifty every man has the face he deserves.* I would say that's true about Nim Chaud, now pastor of Balona's BoMFoG Tabernacle. Reading through the brittle, yellowed pages, he strokes his still-golden Van Dyke.

```
TO   : Cdr. Force Recon Bn
FROM: Exec. 11th ForRecCo
DATE: 02 Dec 68
RE   : Mission Report WEDGE
```

On 30 November 1968 Team Wedge, led by Sgt. E. Breene and including Cpl N. Chaud, L/Cpl A. Bernstein,Pfc D. Keyshot, Pvt F. Vitale, and HC T. Fethering were inserted 0430 at YA168666. Stated mission was: Conduct recon and surveillance in Zone to determine enemy activity. Avoid if possible engaging enemy. Make every effort to capture a prisoner. Plot HLZs for future operations.Pay particular attention to trails and their frequency of use in your RZ. Patrol will not be extracted until RZ is sufficiently covered.
Pvt Vitale who called for extraction 01 Dec was last man standing. Pvt Vitale reports that team saw what appeared by its dress and gear to be the body of a marine lying on the trail near the LZ. Team was unaware of any recent friendly activity in the area. Sgt Breene gave orders to bag the body. L/Cpl Bernstein said he thought it looked like a booby-trap situation, but Sgt

Breene insisted that Bernstein probe the body.
L/Cpl Bernstein advanced and carefully removed
the floppy cover from the head of the body and
discovered the corpse to be that of an old Asian
woman, apparently several days dead. Sgt Breene
signaled the team to advance. The sgt approached
the body and gave it a kick. Evidently a charge
had been set under the body and exploded,
killing Sgt Breene and L/Cpl Bernstein, severely
wounding Pfc Keyshot and Cpl Chaud,superficially
wounding Pvt Vitale, and also seriously
wounding HC Fethering who despite his own wounds
medicated and bandaged Pfc Keyshot,Cpl
Chaud,Pvt Vitale,and himself.
Mission not completed.
Recommendation: Officers and non-coms review SOP
for surveilling and approaching unfamiliar
and/or unusual formations, facilities,
personnel, and ordnance.

Ex-corporal Nimitz MacArthur Chaud leans back in his leather chair, taps my faded folded-refolded scraps, looks puzzled. "How'd you manage to end up with this, Don?"

"You remember Hospital Corpsman Tom Fethering, of course. Well, Feathers wanted me to report Sergeant Breene. Had one of his swabby buddies snitch this copy from battalion. He stuck it in my personal gear that got shipped to Okinawa and then on to Japan. After I got to be more or less human again I figured complaining was useless."

"Would never have done anybody any good." Nim hands the papers to me, folds his large hands, again leans back in his chair, briefly closes his eyes.

I ask, "You ever think about the old days, Herk?"

"Hey, it's been 30 years, Keyhole old buddy. No, more than 30 years."

"Maybe you do think about those ancient times?" We've been addressing each other by our Marine Corps nicknames; that stirs up some memories, too.

2

"I do think about the people—our great guys and their people, and the jungle. Sometimes I recall the sounds and colors of the birds. Much of it I can't remember. The rest I try to forget. A lot of water under the bridge since those days, Don. And a whole lot of new rivers."

I run my fingers through my hair, practically all white now, except for the eyebrows. "I don't think about the people, except those that come back in my dreams. I don't know what I'd say to a Vietnamese today if I ever met one."

I wonder what I would say. There was a Vietnamese girl at Big Baloney, but she would never come in for counseling.

I wonder what I would say to her, what I would feel looking at her face.

Would she know that I killed her father and her uncles and her older brothers and burned her house and destroyed her crops? "I remember hitting the deck frequently, at just about every unexpected sound. And the smell. I remember the smell. You ever want to go back and look?"

"I don't. And you weren't hitting the deck alone."

"You're the only one around here who knows about my situation, besides Mitzi, of course. And Quince Runcible. You and Quince are confidential people, I know. About Mitzi, I really don't know any more."

"Mmm. It's nobody else's business, Don."

"I mean, it's not that I still feel sorry for myself. Really, I don't. I began with having great dreams about changing the world. But lately I've just been trying to discover the person I really am.

"Then, after I think about that, I don't want to find that person, for fear of what I'll reveal. Y'know?"

"Don, I know that for 30 years you've lived a life of service, and people appreciate you. All your students surely appreciated you, still do. Your new clients will appreciate you. I do, too, by the way!"

"Thanks, but I guess what I really wanted to talk about is this." I reach into my shirt pocket and pull out another folded paper, this one of very recent origin. I hand it to Nim.

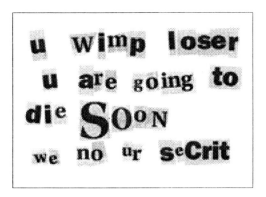

"I found this on the floor under the front-door mail slot this morning."

"Another document!" He holds the paper up to the light, looks at the cut-out and pasted newspaper headline letters comprising the message. "My word! I'm supposing you don't know who put this together?"

"No. I'm not all that much afraid of dying any more, but I'm not thrilled to have people know my secret."

"Mm-hm." He taps the paper. "Oh, Don. This is just somebody who wants to get your goat. The 'I know your secret' is a ploy to disturb, old as the hills. Everybody has secrets, Don; most of them nonsensical, trivial. As a long-time counselor, even as a therapist beginner, you must know that."

"When it's you who's the target it's different, isn't it. You're saying I should forget the threat part." In my head I've been going through my list of complainers, including my two newest male clients who spend their two-person-group hour mostly sneering and bragging about drowning cats, beating up homosexuals, and getting blind drunk.

"Yes. The note's not very specific, is it. Sounds mean. Mean-spirited; it doesn't seem particularly dangerous."

"You're not the one got it, Nim."

"Well, that's true."

"And Lamont's come up missing."

"Your new dog is gone already?"

"I've looked up and down this whole area. Not a sign of him. Maybe the person or persons who pasted up this note took him. Part of the threat."

"Your pooch's been at your place, how long? A couple days is all? Only one day? He may have gone off looking for his old home. I understand dogs will do that, even if their previous home was a disaster."

"He gave every indication that I was his favorite person of all time."

"You got him out of the shelter at a critical time. He surely sensed that."

"Yes. Well. I'm still not sleeping." My need for Nim's advice releases the more urgent reason for my visiting him. "I'm having fantasies. About Mitzi. Dying a bunch of different ways."

"Mmm."

"And sometimes I would like to kill my mother-in-law."

"That's not an uncommon urge, I've heard."

"Don't laugh, Nim. I'm serious. If I took my dreams seriously, I guess they'd say that I'd also like to kill my wife. Both secrets. How could they know my secrets?"

"Mmm. I have an effective contact in Delta City...."

"Is he a vet?"

"No, he's an MD. A psychiatrist. Very competent."

"You're joking again. I meant is he a veteran."

"I know what you meant, Don. I'm trying to lighten us up here."

"It's not to be made light of. Don't smile, Nim. You're always smiling, showing people how happy you are, how satisfied with everything." I feel my voice faltering, hear the whining tone. I hate that nasty tone in my mother-in-law's complaining.

"As a new striver in a mental health profession you surely don't want this low mood to continue."

I can feel my body tensing. "When Breene ordered us forward.... That keeps coming back. That man was an idiot."

"Well, he's dead and gone, Don. He was just one of those rare non-coms who should never have been pro-moted. But all that was a long time ago. A very long time. And he was frightened, a small man out of his depth."

"He didn't like you because of your Navy Cross."

"Probably he was frightened of us because he was considerably less experienced than we were. Perhaps unqualified men who acquire rank are more frightened than the ordinary grunt. Don't you suppose that holds true for all walks of life?"

After a brief silence we both cast our eyes upon the carpet, considering once again the personality and be-havior of Sergeant Breene, Killed In Action thirty years ago and more. I am also considering the personality and behavior of Abel Croon, my ex-principal.

Nim shakes his head, smiles. "It will serve your new clients better if their therapist is exhibiting at least a bit more stability than they. So, about your lost dog, Don. You've given him a name already. What's his name again?"

"Lamont."

Nim smiles. "*The Shadow*. A black dog, of course, and quiet. Comforting to have an ally like that. Ah! You might look into asking young Joseph Kuhl for some help in your search. He's just begun his sophomore year at C4, y'know, and I suspect he would appreciate the encouragement of having an actual flesh-and-blood client." We both chuckle, knowing Joseph Kuhl and his history and ambitions.

C4 is local shortspeak for *Chaud County Community College.* C4 is also an explosive, like Semtex, the compound most likely responsible for Nim's and my historic physical deficits.

"Yes, I'll think about Joseph, too, Nim. Thanks." I flash briefly on a view of Lamont limping his way through rank weeds toward an ancient house with spires, broken steps, and a dead garden. Something out of an old black-and-white movie.

Nim reaches forward and gives my forearm a quick friend-squeeze, the older Balona male's equivalent of a hug. "Don, perhaps you would remember the words of Epictetus: *He is a wise man who does not grieve for the things which he has not, but rejoices for those which he has.* Hm? And best of luck in finding Lamont, Don."

"Yes. Well, I can hope. I'm phoning the shelter soon as I get back to the office; maybe they've picked him up again."

I thank him for helping me get my downtown-Balona office space, which happens to be Nim's old apartment over Mr. D.H. Carp's Groceries & Sundries. "It's shabby but comfortable," he says. "Your clients will feel safe there."

"I may need to move myself up there totally and permanently one of these days."

He gives me a sharp look but does not pursue the subject. We speak of other matters for a few minutes, and as I leave he rises to his full six-foot-seven, not at all favoring his artificial foot. I'm over six feet, but I have to lift my chin to meet his blue gaze. He grasps my oversize hand and it is lost in his grip. "And, by the way, Don, good morning!"

On the way out I notice the legend on Nim's signboard outside Tabernacle: *Who can live and not see death? Who can save himself from the power of the grave? Psalm 89*

Even so, I leave feeling lighter, as if I had paid off a

big bill or had won a small sum on the Lotto or had done someone a favor. Nimitz Chaud does that for everybody.

Chapter Two

Up in my new office I spend some time tidying so that my clients don't have something else to worry about. My first visitor today is not a client, but journalist Bellona Shaw.

"Now, Mr. Crinkle—of course I mean Mr. *Keyshot*—as I mentioned over the phone, this is just for the little piece in our own little Balona *Courier*, to sort of celebrate your recent retirement from Balona High? Of course, I mean recent like last June, y'know. So since this is all so familiar, you don't have to feel nervous, eksedra. So I'll just ast a few questions, and you can answer any way you want. Okay?"

Mrs. Shaw is a long-time Balona resident. Maybe not *very* long-time, but at least longer than I. Although not a member, she regularly attends Tabernacle—sits down in front—and I have met her casually once or twice, perhaps at some school function or other. She is said to be, and speaks like, a lady from New Orleans, except that evidently she has picked up some Balonisms of speech. She is tall, late-forty-ish, pretty in a distinguished way, with pink incipient jowls but no double chin yet, sharp nose and chin, dark eyebrows and eyes, very red lips, pants-suited in blue. This week she's red-haired.

Mitzi complains that Mrs. Shaw is overly proud of her jogging addiction and its affirmative consequences for her figure.

"You're looking at my Adidases? Yas, well, you'll just have to forgive me the informality, sir. They're a very necessary part of my on-going, you might say *continual*

9

self-improvement program, since I'm a runner. No, not a jogger—a *runner!* Yas."

She smiles downwards, brushes a very few imaginary crumblets from her lap, opens her notebook, unscrews her pen. "You're looking at my fountain pen. It's one of those marvellous classics where you actually dip it into a bottle of actual ink and suck up the ink in that way, y'know? Actually!" She holds the pen up for our inspection. "See? Not many around any more. Pens, I mean, not ink. You can still get ink, but you have to look for it. *Law!* So most people nowdays use ballpoints, of course. This handsome black beau is a Mont Blanc, see? I also have a Pelikan, marbled blue, but.... So, now, where were we? Oh, yas. The shoes. No, the pen. Well, let's get beyond that.

"So, Mr. Keyshot, may I call you Don? No, for now I think I'll call you Mr. Keyshot. Sounds more professional, y'know, although Mr. Patrick Preene tells me it's possible you may be joining our little staff, part-time? Is that rumor or conjecture or fact? Since Mr. Patrick Preene himself says so, I'll just take it as fact, and let it go at that. So probably we'll be colleagues one of these days, sort of, and *then* we'll get less formal in our, uh, dialog." She takes a deep breath, her bosom rises precipitously, she bats her eyelashes. "So, now, where were we? Oh, yas. So. Well, what's it like being Miss Mitzi Crinkle's husband?"

Ah. Now we are arriving at the authentic reason for the interview. I should have known. "Well, ma'am, it's an honor and a privilege. What else can one say?"

"My, how gallant!" She writes in her notebook, looks up again. "How gallant! Hmm. You're looking at my pin, here. It's a DOD pin—Daughters of the Delta? Well, actually I'm not a daughter of our local Yulumne Delta, so they cheated for me a bit, since I'm an actual Daughter of the *Mississippi* Delta! It's a pretty pin, though." Mrs. Shaw twists the bauble at her breast so

10

that we may admire it from several angles. "Well, yas, but about how you get along together—that sort of thing. The personal touch. How do you get along about, say, politics?"

"We seldom if ever discuss politics."

"*Law!* How come's that? I should think every happily married couple would discuss politics?" Her eyes are brown, liquid, somehow mournful. Another lonely lady, and it shows. One wishes to be of some assistance to a pleasant creature in evident need. But how, without appearing to be forward, unseemly, *commercial?*

Mrs. Shaw often slows her otherwise rapid speech suddenly and attenuates the words at the ends of sentences. Nimitz Chaud sometimes does that. Nim gives the impression in this way that he's already engaged in formulating his next thought. Perhaps she has learned that from listening to Pastor Nim's sermons. Sounds natural with Nim. "Well then, what do you discuss, Mr. Keyshot?"

"Events of the day. We sometimes discuss events of the day."

"Miss Crinkle—oh, I should say Mrs. Keyshot...."

"'Miss Crinkle' is how she's known far and wide, Mrs. Shaw." I smile, recalling being addressed any number of times—at social events, on the street, over the phone—as *Mr. Crinkle.*

"How she *used* to be known perhaps you mean, since she was so *cruelly* dismissed by those *dreadful* men over at the Delta City television station. *Dreadful* men!" Mrs. Shaw frowns, raises her shoulders and shakes her head rapidly, shudders, reminding me of comedic jowl-wagging imitators of former President Nixon.

"Well, most people still refer to her as 'Mitzi Crinkle'."

"I won't argue that, Mr., uh, Keyshot. So, back to business here." Mrs. Shaw squints her eyes and examines her interviewee closely. "So, how do you manage to absorb that, uh, disprespect?"

The journalist's taunt is designed to stimulate a thoughtless, passionate response—perhaps from a boy. "Oh, I think not disrespect, Mrs. Shaw. Rather, it might be considered respect for a well-known, keenly-missed career personality. One might share in that respect, by reflection."

"How gallant! Yas, of course. How foolish of me." Mrs. Shaw shifts in her chair, looks about, perhaps for signs of coffee or tea. Her eyebrows rise.

"Are you ready for a cup of tea, Mrs. Shaw?"

"Ah!" She reveals peerless dental hygiene and a charming smile. "Call me Bellona."

I rustle about in the kitchenette of this one-room "office" over Mr. D.H. Carp's Groceries & Sundries. Mrs. Shaw enjoys a slice of Audrey Frackle's lemon cake with the tea, a black pekoe tea. Audrey's cake by way of Chum to Mitzi.

I decide to take the initiative. "You must get many questions about your own professional name: Bellona of Balona."

"Tee-hee, law, yes!"

Definitely a pretty lady, Bellona Shaw turns her head to re-do her lipstick, then passes ten minutes describing how it was that she came to Balona back when, and how she acquired her job reporting and commenting on pets, the arts, gardens, and the politics and society of Balona for the *Courier*. "But how I carry on. Law! I came here to get you down in print. And here I am talking about myself. I think it's because you make me nervous, sir!"

I consider the evident loneliness of the woman speaking, and the question slips out: "Have you ever been in counseling, Mrs. Shaw?"

Mrs. Shaw at once rears back in her chair, her eyes open wide, pupils diminished.

"Well, what a question." She pulls her handbag onto her lap, rummages in it.

"I must explain: When it's not only one's pastime, but one's profession, as well as one's consuming interest, then perhaps that's why one becomes so forward, asking such a question. Then, also, many people nowdays unburden themselves liberally, even on the television, with hardly a thought about keeping their private things private. Unburden themselves totally to the millions watching."

"'Many people' maybe; not me." She sniffs. "But that is your new profession, isn't it! My, how well you speak! But of course you were also a teacher, and that's what I thought we were going to talk about. Spanish, was it?"

"And drama and sometimes English when they needed me there. Should've done the French class, too, but they had other ideas. Mostly counseling in recent years, after they dropped the drama program. Never math, though. Never very good at math."

"'...no good at math.'" Her lips frame the words silently as she writes in her notebook. "Yas, now we're getting some facts down. Yas, you speak so well. So, how about education? You went to school where?"

"New Jersey and Delta City. Taught school in New Jersey for a while. Came to Balona to...."

"Balona has its attractions, I know."

Mrs. Shaw spends a few minutes describing her arrival in Balona. Then at last: "And what was it that brought you to Balona?"

"I came because Balona is Pastor Nim Chaud's home town. He and I had become acquainted when we were younger and...."

"Oh, yas, when he was at Yale, yas." She frowns. "I thought Yale was in Massachusetts, not New Jersey. Well, no matter. I learn something new every day. And I dit'n realize you were a Yale man, too."

I let it go. No use to drag in the Corps and the war and the hospitals, and that I never got close to Yale.

13

"So, what kind of exciting things have happened to you? I mean, not only things in your life as a teacher, but also eksedra."

"I was very much excited when I finally finished work for my MFCC license—marriage, family, and child counselor."

"Yas, well I had something more, uh, lively, in mind. For example, about your recent honeymoon. Where, for example, did you take Miss Crinkle, Mrs. Keyshot, on your honeymoon?"

"Mmm. Actually it's not so recent, you know. It's been almost two years now."

"Is that a fact." She writes. "Who was it married you? I mean, well, you know what I mean."

"We were married by Mitzi's lawyer, Judge Kosh Chaud in his chambers in Delta City, immediately following Mitzi's last broadcast and, since she was still concerned about its being her last, and the manner in which her contract was terminated, we came right back here to Balona."

"Oh. Is that a fact. I heard she was really broken up—about getting fired, I mean." *If it bleeds, it leads*, the media people say, but Mrs. Shaw is looking for something jucier, more colorful yet.

"Well, then we went boating on the delta. Sam John Sly said Mitzi could have his yacht for a week, so we took it all the way to San Francisco Bay, tied up at Sausalito, explored that place. Had a nice time."

Mrs. Shaw's face lights up. "How very romantic. Yachting on the delta. In Mr. Sam John Sly's yacht. My!"

"Yes, Mr. Sly's boat is a 42-footer, all the amenities. Would have helped had I been a more expert sailor. Luckily, Mitzi's, ah, Mitzi knew something about it."

Mrs. Shaw is emitting a glow, writing even while keeping her eyes fixed on me, demonstrating that journalistic skill. Her pupils have enlarged.

"Miss Crinkle saved your honeymoon voyage from a disaster?"

"Uh, yes, you could possibly put it that way." For sport I am almost tempted to tease Mrs. Shaw with the information that we had a passenger along who pretty well took over management of the trip as well as the piloting of the boat, but teasing is not my way. And besides, I cannot let that cat out of the bag.

"I understand Miss Crinkle's mother lives with you?"

"A great lady."

"'A great lady...' Mm-hm! Billa Kuhl Runcible Crinkle." Mrs. Shaw squints her eyes at me. She seems to know something about Mother Crinkle's marital history. "I'm not sure everybody in Balona would agree with the 'lady' part of your assessment, would they?"

"A great lady, a perceptive adviser resulting from a long and active life and involvement in community activities."

"I understand you can't drive?"

"I don't care to drive."

"And that you cook divinely."

"I learned a few recipes when I was a student." I'm wondering where she gets her information. Possibly from the ladies at Kute Kurls & Nails, where Mitzi sometimes has her hair done.

"I'll bet your favorite dish is, let me think..." Mrs. Shaw pierces me with a dark flash. "Steak *tartare!*"

Perhaps my facial expression betrays my revulsion.

"Oh. Not steak *tartare.* Then what?"

"I make nice blintzes."

Mrs. Shaw seems not to register the word.

"It's a cream-filled crèpe or pancake? Powdered sugar on top?"

Wimp food, Mitzi says, and fattening.

"Of course. Of course." She writes for a while, looks out the window, thinking. "At that school board meeting last spring, Mr. Abel Croon said some unpleasant things about your performance as a school counselor. Perhaps he was also implying some odd relationships with your students or colleagues. I don't suppose those comments will have any negative effect on your practice as a counselor for adults and families and, uh, children? On your drawing a clientele here in town?"

I feel embarrassment now, and stumble through my response: "As principal of the school, Mr. Croon was under considerable pressure to save money. Eliminating the counseling program was one of his options. As I was the only counselor, I daresay his remarks about the efficacy of counseling have been taken as attacks on me personally. He did phrase a few things somewhat awkwardly. Some people likely were confused. Possibly."

"Well, here's an opportunity to get back at him." Mrs. Shaw has lost her benign expression. "I'll write whatever you say." Her pen is poised.

"I have already said my piece, Mrs. Shaw. What Mr. Croon did was what he felt he had to do. I feel no animosity. None at all. I'm looking forward now to bringing my counseling skills to benefit the people of Balona." I fix my face in the smile that Pippa Burnross, Lawyer Burnross's wife, has identified as my "sweet" smile, the same smile Mitzi describes as "your constipated smile." I'm sure Mrs. Shaw is penning *I feel no animosity.*

She freezes when I ask, "Is there a Mr. Shaw?" She twists her fountain pen shut, plunges it into her handbag, pulls the bag back onto her lap, knees together, a pre-flight position.

"I'm not married, Mr. Keyshot."

"Ah."

"I was married, but I'm not married any more."

"Ah."

However, she does not rise, but stares steadily at the carpet for some time. "I don't usually confide in strangers, but you're not really a stranger, are you? A stranger, but not really. I mean, you are a professional counselor now, right? And happily married youself?"

"In many ways I have a satisfying life."

She mumbles something to herself like, "So it's probably not true about the other thing." And then louder, "Even though Abel Croon said some strange things about you."

I say again, "Mr. Croon was under a lot of pressure and perhaps said things poorly."

"And you are a very discreet person."

"Of course. That's part of the job. Also part of my personality. Almost sphinx-like."

"I mean, you don't tell your wife everything."

"I don't tell my wife *anything* about my clients, or even that a person may be my client." I don't mention that I have only two official clients so far, both bullies and boasters assigned by the court to be cured of a variety of evil habits, young men who would probably be delighted if I shared their "secrets" at Ned's Sportsbar.

"I am being harassed."

"My word. That is typically considered a legal thing. Perhaps you ought to report it to Sheriff Chaud."

"No, no. Not exactly harassed in the accepted sense. It involves that young man, Jess Pleroma. You know Jess Pleroma? Dark, curly hair, white teeth—sharp white teeth—quite attractive in a wild animal sort of way. Remarkable talents. But the way he *looks* at me, y'know?"

"I know who the young man is."

"Oh, I better think about this some more before I talk about it to a veritable stranger. Sorry, I dit'n mean veritable stranger. I meant only that I don't really know you."

"That's true. But you know me better now than you did an hour ago!" I smile showing my clean, non-sharp teeth. It seems to work.

"Law! I came here to interview you, and here I am talking about myself."

"It's an interesting subject." Mrs. Shaw blushes.

"I suppose you have a license and charge a fee."

"Indeed I do. But not exorbitant. Same as counselors in Delta City."

"I suppose maybe I could come up here and talk with you again. I would hope to maybe get some more data on your life. Make it a feature story, eksedra, instead of just items in a column."

"Maybe talk some about what's bothering you."

"Yes. Maybe so." She blushes once again. "Do you know, in your way you are a very handsome man."

She generates little noise on the bare wooden steps down to street level, stairs that usually make the departure of even a lone visitor sound like the passage of a battalion of kindergarteners in full rout. I may have discovered a new client in real need. I feel not only suddenly very handsome, in my way, but—certainly more important—useful. And hopeful. Hopeful. However, Lamont's disappearance worries me. I need to take Nim's suggestion and get some help.

Chapter Three

Young Joseph Kuhl, Balona's only private investigator-in-training, has been trying to live down something of a reputation around town—not with the ladies, but with the law. However, now that Joe is beginning his second year at Chaud County Community College he has pretty well outgrown the sticky-fingers part of his problem, according to the public comments of Joe's cousin Zachary Burnross. In fact, those borderline experiences may even have provided Joe with some insight into the criminal mind. And that should serve him well, his current major academic interest being criminal justice.

Joe is something of a puzzle to most adults around here. He is tall and slim, with wide blue eyes, straight platinum-blond hair, and pink cheeks. The sweet part of his appearance always reminds me of Navy Hospital Corpsman "Feathers" Fethering, a man from my past to whom Nimitz Chaud and I undoubtedly owe our lives. That appearance and attitude proclaims "innocent." The visual association with Feathers overcomes my reluctance to ask for help from Joe Kuhl.

Although Joe has already had some minor commissions as a private eye, including a job assigned by the Balona Town Council, grocer Mr. D.H. Carp represents the opinion of many Balonans that perhaps Joe is proceeding in life not so much innocent as merely one brick short of a normal load.

So, one wonders just what Joe's "private investigations" are likely to turn up. But perhaps in the spirit of friendship his involvement in my project is worth a try.

Nim Chaud is convinced that Joe is good-hearted and that he will turn out "just fine." Of course, Nim has good opinions about nearly everyone, even about Bellona Shaw's sharp-toothed admirer Jess Pleroma who still lurks in various Balona by-ways when he's not in jail, and is said to be an "evil companion" if ever there was one.

Joe's office being immediately across Front Street from the estimable Peking Peek-Inn, the smell of stir-fried vegetables is tantalizing. With Nim's recommendation in mind, I cross the street and enter

Kenworth O. Kuhl Real Estate
and
Joseph Oliver Kuhl
Private Investigations

The odor of moist dog is heavy in the office air. "Hello, Kenworth! How's things? I was sorry to miss you at the last Solidarity breakfast, Kenworth. I hope all is fine with you."

Kenworth Kuhl, Joe's dad, looks sleepy as he raises his head from evident desktop slumber. His red dog Killer rises slowly from beneath Kenworth's desk, stretches and yawns. Kenworth stifles a yawn. "Yeh, how's things? Well, I had a sort of emergency at home." It might accurately be said that Kenworth often has emergencies at home.

"I hope all is well."

"Well, sort of well, you don't count Bapsie. Bapsie was practicing in the driveway again and drove the car smack into the garage door is all." Bapsie—Mrs. Kenworth Kuhl—is infamous in Balona for having the combination of weak eyes, enormous physical strength, a foul mouth, and execrable driving habits, not to speak of no driver's license and off-road road-rage. That is an uncharitable description. Despite my 20-odd years of residence in Balona, I have never had reason to speak to the woman since her years at Balona High. I suppose she must have developed into a fine person beneath it all, except that perhaps her drinking habits may obscure some of her finer qualities.

Kenworth elaborates: "Actually, she hit *next* to the garage door. Give it quite a powerful smash, so the building got sort of pushed in, you might say. And then we cut'n open the garage door or the side door to the house, either one. I had to call Binky Swainhammer to come over and try and fix it all, and Binky showed up without his tools. 'I just come over to see what was what,' he went. And so then I had to wait around, y'know, for him to come back with his sledgehammer and stuff. So."

Kenworth rubs his finger at a scratch in his desktop. His voice falls, the word coming slow, extending the s, "Sorry."

"Well, I came looking for Joseph."

"Oh, gee. Did Joey do something bad?"

"I was hoping maybe he could help find someone for me."

"Jeez! You'd hire Joey to do that? You think he could do that?" I don't hear an enthusiastic paternal recommendation ringing through these queries.

"Will he be in today? I thought it being Saturday, he might be at your office."

"Joey's went and took himself across the street to have some lunch. I ate mine quick, but he's probably talking to Millie Wong over there. You know, the little girl goes to school with him, and her dad owns the place?"

"Maybe I'll go on over there and meet with him there."

"He's eating chop suey probably. Takes him an hour when he's talking, too. Puts a lot of soy sauce on it. Say, did you happen to see a big magpie sitting up on the roof here when you come in? Big one?"

"Can't recall seeing a magpie, no."

"I mean, you cut'n miss him if he was there. Sometimes he's there; sometimes he's not. Well, anyways, how come *you're* looking for somebody?" Kenworth's pale face at once reddens. "Oh, that's probably protected by parent-client privilege, something like that? I shut'n ask a question like that. I should know better." Kenworth's head droops. Killer's head droops.

"It's probably a minor thing that will work itself out, but I hope Joseph might be able to help resolve it more quickly. Maybe Killer will be able to help, too."

Kenworth appears to have suddenly acquired a major headache. He closes his eyes.

So I let him in on my plans. "I got a dog from the shelter over in Delta City, Kenworth, but the dog's disappeared I don't know where, and I want to find him before he slides into the river or gets run over or something else bad happens to him. He's an older dog. Joseph may be able to help with something like this, don't you think?" I flash briefly on Lamont struggling in the chill waters of the Yulumne, caught in the current, swept along, unable to reach the other bank. Lamont turns his head, looks back, terrified.

"A dog. Well, I think maybe Joey is pretty interested in catching spies and solving major crimes, but since there's probably no major spies or crimes around Balona today that I know of, he might be able to help with a dog. Yeh. Maybe so. I hear a lot of dogs are gone missing lately. Not Killer, though. Killer sticks with me like ticks on a dog. Anyways, good luck with your quest. And nowdays all my friends call me 'Kayo' instead of 'Kenworth,' okay?" Kenworth lays his head down on his arm, closes his eyes. Killer collapses with a thump under Kenworth's desk, closes his eyes.

I believe I have been dismissed, but respond I hope appropriately on exiting, "Okay, Kayo."

As the usual lunch hour has expired, the Peking Peek-Inn is nearly empty of customers. Very tall and muscular owner Mr. Benjamin Wong is wiping the counter. He smiles at me, raises his towel in greeting. There is sudden clangor in the kitchen, then silence, except for the KDC-FM golden oldies emanating from the radio next to the cash register. Joseph Kuhl sits at the counter, an almost-empty plate before him. He is closely occupied with an electronic device that emits beeps as he massages it with his thumbs.

"Hello, Joseph. Your dad said you might be here. How's things?"

He looks up. "Huh? Hello, there Mr. Keyshot. How's things?"

"Yes. A new calculator?"

"Nah. It's sort of a video game without you plug it in to the TV, see? I'm up to 5,000 points and if I can get 10,000 points it plays a special tune. I think. I been playing it all day and never been up there yet." Joe frowns; the instrument beeps several times without any thumb-work. "Dumb thing. Belongs to my cousin Zack, only his dad gets mad when he sees Zack playing with it, so Zack gave it to me. Sort of gave it. What I mean is, Zack doesn't really ever give anything, even to a blood relative."

"You're not working at Mr. D.H. Carp's today."

"Uh-huh, right. I, uh, got a sore back, or throat, one or the other."

"You finished here, Joseph?:"

"Uh, just a minute, Mr. Wong." Joe picks up his chopsticks and with a few expert snicks finishes his lunch. "There you go." Joe licks off his chopsticks and stuffs them into the pocket of his leather jacket. Joe frowns, looks up. "You said you just seen, saw my dad, did you? He said something about a magpie, did he?"

"He mentioned something. Yes, he asked if I saw a magpie up on the roof over there. I told him no."

"He sees that old bird whether it's there or not, y'know."

"I didn't know that." Ah, another potential client. But perhaps a psychiatric case. Mr. Wong approaches with raised eyebrows, a smile, and a menu. "I'm just here to see Joseph, Mr. Wong, so I won't be dining today."

"I've meant to tell you, Mr. Keyshot. We really appreciate all you've done for Amelia. She got invited to DU's Conservatory because of you. She'd have gone there, too, except that she really wants to go into law enforcement. Anyways, thanks."

"Well, Mr. Wong. If she keeps up her piano work she will have something additional to enjoy throughout her life."

"I just wanted to make sure you understand we appreciate you—even if certain others maybe don't." Mr. Wong resumes his chores.

"You come to see me? I mean, *me*?" Joe puts his device on the counter, watching it out of the corner of his eye, as if unattended it might creep away.

"I thought you might be able to provide me with some assistance."

"You mean give you some help?"

"Exactly what I meant."

"How could I help you? What I mean is, you're the guy usually helping other guys."

"Now don't laugh, but I need help to find my new dog."

Joseph doesn't quite snort. He obviously holds it back. "Oh. Well, I know a lot of Balona dogs have came up missing lately, but I don't do dogs, Mr. Keyshot. What I mean is, I'm a private investigator does people, y'know. Not exactly got a real license yet, but I do got an expert-type background in investigation procedures, and I already solved some crimes, even though I guess nobody around here is ready to admit it. What I mean is, I'm looking into getting me a Beretta nine millimeter with a shoulder holster and extra clips." Joe lowers his eyelids as he reveals these facts, creates a passable imitation of Robert DeNiro confiding something poten-tially criminal. On the other hand, Joe looks quite a bit like his father, including the pointed ears, except that Joe is taller, has more hair and general color, and seems more responsive, more alive. Also possibly more violence-prone.

"Maybe I should have said 'old dog' instead of 'new dog.' He's maybe seven or eight years old, and I'm wor-ried. I thought perhaps you could borrow your dad's dog and we could go out searching, sniffing around." I flash on a *Courier* story of a few years ago about bea-ver-trapping pioneers having lived nearby. I suffer briefly an image of Lamont, his foreleg caught in a bea-ver trap hidden among the exposed willow roots on the banks of the Yulumne. Lamont gnaws on his leg to free himself. I search my pocket for an aspirin.

Joe responds: "Uh. Well, Killer likes squirrels a lot. What I mean is, he sniffs around a squirrel and you can kiss your dog-search goodbye. That's all he's inter-ested in." Joe frowns, thinking. "But Zack's got a dog now. Harley? Harley's pretty smart. What I mean is, maybe you could get Zack and Harley to help." Joe searches in his jacket, pulls out a small black cell-phone. "I'll call him up and see if he's busy." Joe presses keys, listens, presses keys again, listens, bangs the phone on the counter and listens again. "Well, fooey! Dumb thing. Battery's probably dead again. Anyways, Zack's pretty much a grinch. What I mean is, he wut'n do it for nothing."

"Oh, I expect to be charged a fee for services."

Joe's face lights up. "Oh, yeh? I thought maybe this was a charity case. You know, you being a Tabernacle volunteer employee and all. And what with you getting kicked out of Balona High. Uh. What I mean is, I might be able to squeeze you in my schedule. Uh, how much you figure the job's worth?"

"What's your rate, Joseph?"

"Well, it's a hundred a day, plus expenses."

I must have registered shock, for he at once revises his estimate. "Of course, for sort of pro-bono work like this, I would go for, maybe, ten dollars?"

"Ten dollars for the job."

"Yeh, or an hour. Whatever."

"Being still mostly on a teacher's pension, I'm afraid I couldn't go ten dollars an hour."

"I could do it for ten dollars, period, but you'd have to negotiate separate with Zack. What I mean is, Zack's a real grinch. Never does any job pro-bono like me. Which I do sometimes. When I'm not real busy. And when it's a guy I like, y'know." His brows knit. "You're sort of a psychologist now, right? What I mean is, you used to be only a school counselor, but now you been fired, you took up private practice, like?"

"I think you have been disabused about my being fired, Joseph."

"Oh, yeh?" He frowns.

"I have retired is all."

"Uh-huh." Joe doesn't look convinced. "Well, I never been abused, actually, you don't count my ma beating on me. What I mean is, it's not really countable, since she beats on all of us, equal opportunity, y'know?"

"I see. Yes, well, I'm not a licensed psychologist. But I am a licensed mental health therapist, you might say—a family counselor."

"Hey, yeh! Maybe you could come counsel my family." He suddenly looks worried. "No. I guess not. My ma would have a fit and probably bust you up just for looking at her funny the way you do."

I make a mental note to review in the mirror various of my facial expressions. One cannot be too careful about facial expression, I know, having simply smiled pleasantly at he antics of some boisterous French Camp fishermen in Ned's Sportsbar one evening, immediately after which Ned had to rescue me.

"So, Joseph, will you at least think about helping me out?"

"Maybe it's Jess got him. Jess is always swiping stuff and selling it at the fleamarket over in Delta City."

"Jess."

"Jess Pleroma. That Jess. The creep. I guess you don't remember Jess from Big Baloney. He was maybe already expelled when you came to town?"

"I know who he is, but I don't think...."

Joe looks at me intently, interrupts. "What I was just thinking before Jess. What I mean is, my Cousin Nim—you know, Pastor Nim Chaud—he once mentioned that he thought psychologists and counselors, those kind of guys, they are all sort of headed for the looney-bin themselves, and that's why they go into their way of making a living. Learn how to help themselves out first. Y'know?" Joe's cheeks flame. "What I mean is, I'm actually sort of a psychologist myself, y'know, so some guys think I'm sort of weird. What I mean is, even I think I'm sort of weird."

I wait.

His voice lowers and his head swivels to the right and then to the left and back again. "What I mean is, I'm still trying to figure out what I'm doing about investigations, eksedra, y'know? So, if I take the job, maybe you'll give me some pointers about how to get over weirdness, and I could give you some pointers about the current and on-going investigation, and like that. Y'know?"

"Yes. We could share observations and hypotheses."

"Hypotheses, yeh. Like that." He frowns. "And that way I wut'n have to charge you so much, you being crippled up the way you are."

I freeze. I can feel myself freezing up, loins first, as usual, then abdominals, then chest, and finally, jaw and lips. I force a breath and quiver an exhalation. "What do you mean, "crippled?"

27

"Well, you know. Like, I heard you got crippled up in the war over there a long time ago."

My laugh is forced. "Ha ha. Do I have an odd walk? A limp? Where in the world did you hear that?"

"Oh, I don't know. Maybe Patella, Patella Sackworth? You remember Patella from Big Baloney, writes a column for the *Courier?* She knows a lot about guys from listening to the ladies talking over at Kute Kurls & Nails while she sweeps up over there. Maybe she said something. What I mean is, maybe you're not crippled up at all. I just meant. You know."

I decide to change the subject. "I'm getting myself ready to write a column for the *Courier* now, too, you know. So I know Miss Sackworth and her grandfather, Mr. Patrick Preene. Uh, do I look crippled to you?"

"No, I guess not. Well, sort of. What I mean is, maybe it's you just *look* crippled, give the impression, like."

"Ah. Well, we learn something new about ourselves every day—if we have a perceptive observer around." I smile. Mitzi says I look sick when I smile. *You should show your teeth when you smile; otherwise you look constipated.* I show my teeth. "So, do you think you'll be able to help me out?"

"About the old dog? Sure. Uh, I usually get an advance on my fee." Joseph shuffles his feet, looks embarrassed.

"No problem. Here." I dig out a five-dollar bill which he snatches and stuffs in his jacket without looking at it. "On account."

"Okay. Well, where you think we oughtta start?"

"Well, Joseph, I thought that you being the detective might give *me* some clues."

I show my teeth again.

"Okay. Well, then. Since I got some important business to clean up first, let's start tomorrow. Say around 11:00AM in the morning. What I mean is, that'll give us some time to think about stuff."

"That's almost another entire day Lamont is on his own in a strange place, Joe. Maybe he's lying injured somewhere."

"Oh. Yeh. Well. So, okay. How's about 8:00AM."

"How about 300:PM."

"Tomorrow."

"Today, this afternoon."

"I thought you do psychology now? Uh, family stuff."

"No clients this afternoon."

"Oh. Well, okay."

"I'll meet you in front of your office?"

"Yeh. See you then." Joe hands Mr. Wong the five-dollar bill and pockets the change, smiles at me. "I get the full fee irregardless, right?"

"Right."

"Okay! What's good for business is good for me!"

Chapter Four

All that I have described thus far transpired from this morning up to about 1:30. Since then I have been considering how to proceed. When I consider, I talk to myself. People talk to themselves all the time. My clients all admit to doing it. Trouble is, they do it the same way they talk to their wife or their barber or their post-person. That is, they talk at the person. The trick is to talk *with* oneself, have a meaningful conversation. In the as-yet few hours since the friendship began between Lamont and me, I have found that I can have a more meaningful conversation with him than with most humans.

It's not so difficult as it may sound. After I brought him home yesterday—it was in mid-afternoon—Lamont spent all his time watching me, looking at me. He lay there on the living room carpet, his head on his paws, his brown eyes cast up at me where I sat in my chair reading, occasionally sqeaking a move among the leather cushions, sighing, coughing. I would glance over at him and smile. I swear he would smile back. At least his mouth and eyes and general expression appeared to change: a twinkle here, a twitch there. Also the eyebrows would move. The eyebrows are what make much of the difference.

Having Lamont with me for only a few hours had already made a great deal of difference in an otherwise uneventful life. Such changes often affect persons and events profoundly, and far out of proportion to one's original estimates. Before beginning my practice I had thought that the lives of my clients would be eventful, soul-stirring, with gut-wrenching problems to probe (and me to help ameliorate). It was certainly so in my observations during my training to become a therapist. It is certainly so in the literature of therapy.

But I have already discovered that the lives of my clients are much as mine appears to be on its surface—uneventful—and their troubles are compendia of minor irritations. They have no major monsters expressible yet. Only irritations. Irritation with the way a spouse masticates his or her breakfast, irritation with the personal odors of others, irritation with traffic, with noises.

It is these minor irritations compounded that appear to drive people to distraction.

I wondered if my own monsters might somehow be construed as irritations. No, probably not. I questioned Lamont.

"Why, Lamont, is it considered so important to have children?"

Lamont responded, "It is important for one reason alone: to perpetuate the race."

"Well, others handle that just fine. Some of our Balona families actually over-produce."

"Yes, I have relatives who do that. My own sire produced offspring in the hundreds, I am sure. Nevertheless, there it is."

I believe we could have gone on this way for hours, I proposing; he disposing, or at least arguing. But then we heard Mitzi's Green Giant in the driveway.

She slammed the front door.

Her irritations were in bloom.

"What's that stink! Where did you pick *that* up?"

"He's been in a shelter for a week where nobody really took care of him." Mitzi could not possibly have smelt Lamont, for Lamont has no odor to speak of. I have extraordinarily keen olfactory powers. Lamont is an odorless dog.

"Well, you cut've taken it over to Fring's and had Kenny give it a bath before you brought it in here. What's Mother going to think?"

Mother Crinkle was at the moment still participating in one of Bapsie Kuhl's extended bridge games and drinking parties.

"I'll take him into the bathtub and..."

"Not in my bathtub you won't. You can take it out into the backyard and squirt it with a hose. And then give it a shot of Clorox. That should fix the smell for a while. And then you can leave it out on the back porch."

"Mitzi, it's November."

"So? I won't have a stinking creature like that in my house. Ugh!"

Lamont had turned himself so that he was looking at the wall, both ears up, obviously listening carefully.

"Well, I ...."

"And just remember whose house this is, will you."

How could I forget.

"I can build him a lean-to tomorrow, on the sunny side of the garage. Since you keep it locked anyway and never put the Green Giant in there, I could cut a hole in the side wall there so he can go into the garage when the weather begins to turn really cold, colder."

"You're not cutting a hole in my garage."

"Ah. Well, then, I'll get Binky Swainhammer to build him a nice insulated house, in the back yard. Maybe with a little heater in it."

"Where in the back yard exactly do you propose to place such an eyesore when I'm planning my winter garden party out there in only three weeks? My god, a 'little doghouse with a heater in it.' What're you gonna come up with next!"

"Out of the way, of course." Mitzi's winter garden party was rained out last year. Could be rained out again this year.

"It'll poop all over the grass, and my guests'll get dog-doo all over their shoes. Yechh."

"There's mostly gravel and stones out there, Mitzi. And anyway I'll clean up after him. He'll be neat; he's a neat dog; he's not a cow, after all."

"Well, a cow would probably smell a whole lot better...and give milk and butter and eggs as well. Get it out of here! Chum's coming over right away maybe with that cute Jess-boy who wants to buy the Giant, and Mother will be back soon, too, and I don't want them to gag when they come in." Mitzi swept off toward the bathroom, strewing scarf and handbag and gloves and coat on the way. She stopped in the doorway. "Why cut'n you get a parrot or something? A stuffed parrot would suit you nicely." She turned and disappeared. Lamont looked at me, an eyebrow raised, his lip curled.

"Yes, you don't have to say it, Lamont. We'll just establish bivouack on the back porch, you and I."

I must here reveal that my bedroom was once Mitzi's father's bedroom and still includes a large sepia portrait of that fellow hanging on the wall. It's positioned so that the first thing one must see upon awakening is the visage of Absalom Crinkle at age 70.

"Where else in that room would you hang it?" This from Mitzi when I remarked that I was about to remove the portrait and replace it with a personal choice, a Monet print perhaps.

"Well, I'd just put him up in the closet."

"No. That's Daddy. He stays right there. Mother doesn't want him in her room. She still prefers Mousy Runcible, I guess, even after all these years. I wut'n feel comfortable having Daddy in my room following me with his eyes like that all the time. He was more than a little strange that way when he was alive, I guess I never mentioned. So you get to keep him where he is. Just get used to him."

Mitzi is a New Woman. That was that.

So with Lamont banished from Mitzi's Daddy's bedroom, Lamont and I investigated the possibilities of the back porch. I set up my summertime backyard camp cot and the kerosene heater I bought on sale from Mr. D.H. Carp's Groceries and Sundries for just-in-case reasons. I hauled from the garage attic into the porch the empty carton Mitzi's new computer monitor had been packed in (saved just-in-case), cut a hole in it, and padded it with an old blanket. Lamont poked his head into the box, pronounced it appropriate, and disappeared within. We thus spent last night satisfactorily, although I missed my ten o'clock TV news. Having taken a pill to aid slumber, I slept deeply. As I drifted off I could hear Lamont snoring, an older dog's contented buzz, I thought. But as of this morning Lamont was not to be found, thus my conferences earlier today with Nimitz and then with Joseph Kuhl.

Three o'clock and I'm sitting in the office of Kenworth Kuhl and Joseph Oliver Kuhl, chatting with Mr. D.H. Carp. Mr. Carp's grocery store (with my new office above it) is across the street and down the block. Kenworth "Kayo" Kuhl is not present. Joseph is not present. Mr. Carp is obviously irritated, perhaps a potential therapy client.

"He's supposed to work at my place on Saturdays, cleaning up, stocking shelves, helping out, eksedra. Not much good for anything else, since he's always thinking about something else." Mr. D.H. Carp is complaining about Joseph Kuhl's absence. "Today I guess he forgot about me totally."

"It must be irritating." I am practicing my therapeutic dialogue.

"It's more than irritating. I'd like to strangle him, stupid kid. I pay him good wages and he doesn't even bother to show up. I should fire him on the spot."

"You're thinking about firing him."

"I just said that."

"Yes. Well."

"Say, it's true about you getting fired over at the high school, isn't it."

"No. What's true is that I retired." The therapeutic session is evidently concluded.

"Well, everybody says that's what you'd say, but actually they fired you." He fixes me with his pale stare, very similar to the gaze of Mother Crinkle when she thinks she's caught you in some evil endeavor. "Fired you for some secret reason nobody is willing to talk about. I used to be on the school board, y'know. I know about that stuff they do for secret reasons, eksedra."

"I believe your information in this instance is not accurate, Mr. Carp. I simply retired when the board decided they weren't going to support counseling any more."

"You like boys."

"I like boys and girls both."

"Ah! One of those." He relaxes his posture, softens his glare, licks his thin lips, appears more sympathetic. "I could tell you a few things, y'know, about Balona people who like boys and girls. One of them used to own this building. Mr. Oliver Kuhl? He liked girls. Mr. Putzi Purge—the man got himself murdered over in Delta City? Mr. Putzi Purge liked boys. You say you like boys." Mr. D.H. Carp leans forward as if to capture my essence.

"I said I like boys *and* girls. I'm a teacher, Mr. Carp. Show me the teacher who doesn't like boys and girls and I'll show you a failure as a teacher. And probably a failure as a human being."

Mr. D.H. Carp's body language exhibits first surprise, then disappointment. "Oh. Well, I wasn't talking about liking them *that* way. Well, never mind."

Mr. D.H. Carp appears uncomfortable again, tense. "I wonder where that stupid boy could be."

"I wonder where Father Kenworth could be, leaving his office unattended this way."

"Kenworth usually goes over to Fring's Bowls in the afternoon between one and three. Mid-morning, too, usually. Stretches out in a booth over there. Takes a couple long naps. Famous for that, y'know. Everybody knows that." Mr. D.H. Carp frowns, shakes his head at my ignorance. I wonder if Mr. D.H. Carp cuts headline letters out of newspapers.

Joseph suddenly pops into the office, jangling the bell over the door, causing his two waitpersons to jump. I observe, "Ah. Well, here's our young man."

"Oh-oh. I got a temporary strain in my back, Mr. Carp, so what I mean is, I figured you wut'n want me hanging around groaning, eksedra, depressing the customers and not being able to carry stuff out to cars, and like that. Uh, that's why you're over here, I guess?"

"You cut've phoned and told me. I cut've got young Jess Pleroma to fill in. He come in earlier, looking for a job. I had to remind him the job's filled. Hah! Instead, I got to carry stuff out to cars myself, since Piggy's got a sore back, too. Again." Piggy Sackworth is Mr. D.H. Carp's assistant at D.H. Carp's Groceries & Sundries. It suddenly occurs to me that the "cute Jess-boy" Mitzi referred to recently might well be Jess Pleroma, famous for mysterious acquisition and disposition of the automobiles of a number of gullible Balona women. Perhaps I should warn Mitzi.

Joseph appears unconcerned about Mr. D.H. Carp's plight. He turns on his computer and sits watching the screen while the machine loads. "I got a client I'm trying to assist, Mr. Carp, so—what I mean is—along with the sore back and the client, I guess I won't be able to show up today." He opens his eyes very wide and smiles at Mr. Carp softly with his lips closed. With the pale hair floating about his head and his wide blue eyes, he suddenly looks like an illuminated illustration of a sacred figure in a religious tract.

Mr. D.H. Carp drinks in the effect. His expression changes from irritation to borderline adoration. "Well, Joseph, I hope you're feeling better soon." He sighs, rises, gives me what might be a significant look, leaves without another word.

"So, now, Mr. Keyshot. Where you want to start looking for this dog? Like, on the street outside? What I mean is, we could go take a walk and whistle and call him, and like that."

"I don't have a car, Joseph, and I have heard of your famous *Yellow Peril*. So could we check the roads for a few miles out of town, both toward Delta City and elsewhere? I'm worried that maybe he might have been hit by a car or a truck and is lying by the side of a road somewhere near." I flash briefly on Lamont on the side of a road, victim of a mine or booby trap, black blood and flies.

Joseph appears suddenly to present symptoms of depression. "Well, about the car, what I mean is, I haven't drove my Yellow Peril for a while, so I don't know if the battery's dead or there's any gas or what."

"We can stop by Fring's and fill up first."

Joseph's face brightens. "Yeh. Well, all right!"

It is only a two-long-block walk to Joseph's house and we arrive there well before 3:30. Joe's yellow car is parked on the street, the doors unlocked, the keys visible, dangling from the sunshade on the driver's side.

Joe explains the vulnerable keys: "Gas is so expensive I keep forgetting I even got a car." The vehicle starts immediately and we fill up at Fring's Service on Airport Way.

Hanky Fring, Doctor Fring's only child, serves us by standing in the doorway of the office, observing. "Get it yourself, Joe, and you drive off without paying, just remember I got your license plate number and also am good friends with Junior Trilbend."

"Well, fooey! Mr. Keyshot here is gonna pay, so don't get all pushed out of shape. It was a simple oversight." Evidently there is history here.

I pay, awarding Hanky a dollar bill for his trouble. Hanky stares at the bill as if it might be counterfeit. "You hanging out with Mr. Keyshot now, Joey?" Hanky eyes me narrowly.

"Mr. Keyshot is my client."

"We're looking for a medium-size dark-brown dog with one pointed ear upstanding, the other flopped down. Have you perhaps seen him around here? Short tail? Like maybe he's at your daddy's place?" Hanky Fring's daddy is Doctor Kenworth Fring, DVM

"I don't know what Daddy's picked up lately, if any-thing, but mostly he's been watching football and drinking beer. Now, I seen a little black dog with two ears sticking up all right, but he belongs to Zack Burn-ross, and Zack was on a skateboard and had him on a leash pulling. Name's Harley. Zack named him after a motorsikkle. Makes sense."

Hanky's motorcycle is parked next to the office door. Hanky leans over and wipes at the machine tenderly with a blue bandana. "Motorsikkles are suave." He looks at Joseph's yellow sedan. "And they don't use much gas, either."

Joe ignores this comment. "I guess we'll go out Air-port Way for a while, look at the side of the road for bodies, eksedra."

And so we do, travelling toward Delta City, each of us examining the weeds at the shoulders of the road carefully for signs of Lamont.

"How come you named him Lamont. That after a friend of yours?"

"Lamont was a character in a radio drama when I

was a boy. Seemed an appropriate name."

"What's a radio drama."

"Before TV was so universal, that's what we had to amuse us. Stories you listened to, with actors taking the parts of various characters."

"Oh, like *As the World Turns*."

"That, too, but not quite. Drama, even music, but no pictures."

"Sounds dumb."

"Anything but. You had to use your imagination to figure out what the scene and the characters looked like."

"I guess you dit'n have cars, either, in those olden days, so that's how come you don't know how to drive."

I think about the history curriculum at Balona High School, the preoccupations of the faculty, the difficulty young people have of considering any history but their own, the odd interests of modern youth, the psychology of the adolescent, and a variety of other things before commenting.

I decide not to comment.

Instead I suggest, "Maybe we could get to the Interstate and drive back to where the West Levee Road meets it, and come back that way, maybe go out east."

"Okay." And so we do. A few dead hawks on the shoulders of the Interstate, products of primeval hawkish tunnel vision meeting the monstrous bulk and speed of modern bigrigs. On the West Levee Road, we see roadkill that includes dead squirrels, skunks, raccoons as accidental victims or deliberate targets; and the occasional pheasant that didn't move fast enough. No dogs today. No bodies to bag.

I think about the jungle and all the birds and the insects. And death. I can still smell Vietnam. Why don't the memories go away? The memories of other combat veterans leave them, some quickly, they say. Why not mine? My scars ache. I dig out an aspirin and chew it.

"You taking dope now?" Joe hasn't taken his eyes off the road, but he's watching me.

"It was an aspirin."

"Uh-huh. My ma eats 'em for breakfast when she's had too much toddy."

"I try to limit my intake."

"You wanna try the East Levee Road, too, right?"

We continue past Balona, roofs in various states of repair visible down below the levee, past Tabernacle's blue tile roof and the high school stadium berm at eye level (graffiti from Fruitstand High visible on the press box), past the dump and the cemetery. After five miles Joseph eases his car into the gravel. "You wanna go on?"

"I think we'd have seen some evidence if he'd been hit by a car on any of these roads. I guess either he got picked up by animal control again or he's still somewhere in Balona." Or—I flash on Lamont struggling through those weeds again, on his way to some nameless destination, focused, weary, determined.

"Well, I guess I did my part of the job okay, okay?" Joseph keeps turning his head my way, possibly hinting about his five-dollar remainder. "I guess you can recommend me for investigative work, Mr. Keyshot, huh?"

"Sure. I guess so." I hand him another fiver and at my driveway wave goodbye as his yellow car disappears.

Chapter Five

The Green Giant isn't in the driveway when I am delivered. Giant is Mitzi's Jaguar, and his absence means I'm home before Mitzi for once. Mitzi refers to the Giant as "him" rather than "her" or "it," something I have come to find instructive. A hand-printed Chumnote is pinned to a crevice in the front door:

> *Love, I'll meet you at six and we can have a nice run and whatever afterwards. We can talk about the rally. C*

Mitzi's friend Chum Kleebnock is a teacher at Balona High. I have heard Chum's given name is "Juliet," but no one ever calls her anything but Chum. Chum and Mitzi hit it off right away when Mitzi and I were in our very brief dating phase last year—or was it two years ago—and I took Mitzi to one of the faculty wine-and-cheese parties Audrey Frackle throws for paid-up union members every quarter or so. On that occasion Chardonnay-full Chum at once selected Mitzi, and the two of them danced cheek to cheek for some time, creating quite a stir among the faculty.

Chum and Audrey have lived together for years, everyone says, but since Chum has taken up with Mitzi—Chum navigating for the sportscar rallies that Mitzi drives—Audrey appears to have been sort of pushed aside, perhaps only temporarily. Audrey frowns at me whenever she sees me, probably blaming me for her loss. I wonder if Audrey is vindictive. I wonder if she cuts letters out of the newspaper.

I remove the pin and leave it alongside the note face-up on the hall table next to the mail—credit card bills again, with *Important, Open Immediately* printed in large red letters all over the envelopes. Mitzi's debits. I use only cash, finding credit cards possibly addictive and wishing to avoid that trap.

I hang up my coat, wonder about where last spring I stored my scarf and my beret. Students and colleagues used to laugh at that beret, but it's warm and comforting. It's beret weather now. In the hall mirror I notice once again that my hair is phasing toward total white. Only the eyebrows have much color. Even the eyelashes are paling. And the skin is wrinkled, more yellow than pale. I'm wondering if my medication could have anything to do with it, if perhaps it needs to be increased. I'd blame Agent Orange except that Dad acquired much the same coloration early on.

From Joseph's car we had heard geese honking their way south, probably stopping for sustaining snacks in the delta. Even with daylight-savings time gone it's dark at five, and six will be pitch black. I can't imagine any pleasure in jogging the streets of Balona in the cold and dark, like a boot at Parris Island before morning mess. Who was it said, "Life is a rose garden: the petals wilt, the thorns remain"? Probably Fritz Perls or Harry Peace. Mitzi's friend Chum has to keep her famous muscles in trim, thus her jogging. And "running keeps me in shape," says Mitzi. "I'll have to be in shape if I ever expect to get on the tube again."

Mitzi does two or three auditions a month, sometimes more, all over the north state. She's been trying to get back into the television business since the day she was fired. But once you've been fired, and then off the air for a year, who will hire you?

"I need something dramatic in my life. Something that'll get their attention," she has said several times. Maybe that's why the frantic rallies. I want to hug her, kiss her, snuggle with her, make ingenious, creative love to her. I do love her.

I should probably tell her again. I did so last year. "I don't like that stuff," was her response. I can only continue to hope.

Mother Crinkle is in the living room, watching a gameshow on the TV. "Hi, Mother Crinkle!"

"Hush! I'm watching my show. Don't bother me. Dammit, Dan, you always do that. You always bother me when I'm watching my shows. It's hard enough trying to hear what Teddy's saying there without someone always interrupting when you're trying to hear."

"It's the commercial playing now, Mother Crinkle. In fact, it appears to me that the show is now over." I smile—pleasantly, I hope—showing my teeth.

Mother Crinkle rearranges the pillows on the couch, pummeling them with remarkable force and expressing irritation that *someone* has moved them from the way she likes them. She has her own room with its own pillows, appliances and complex arrangements, but she likes it here. She settles herself, points across the room.

"As long as you've interrupted me you might as well sit, Dan." It should be noted that established Balonans consider it rude to point with the finger. They use the thumb instead, holding that polite pointer out from the body as if to sight-in a mortar or press an elevator button or celebrate a victory. Mother Crinkle aims at my usual chair, maintains the elevation of her arm and cants the pointing thumb until I comply.

"So, Dan. Miriam finally tells me you're not gonna make babies with her, finally tells me after all these years. Three years, is it now." Mother Crinkle often mispronounces my name. When about to make a moral-type judgment, she often refers to Mitzi by her given name, so I brace myself. "You sure ought to know Miriam's fast getting beyond the age where she can have babies easy at all? That's a fact, well, I had six, you don't count...well, never mind, and I myself was getting along when Mitzi arrived, because we all had babies in those days, since that's how you populate the world with decent people, where the decent people are the ones must have the babies, y'know, since otherwise the low-lifes will have all the babies and run the show, so you never figured that out? I figured that out when I was practically a kid. I had Mitzi when I was over fifty years old, that's how dedicated I was, doesn't get easier. Dedicated, I was, but threw up practically all the time with her, so she was the last one."

Mother Crinkle was born Wilhelmina Kuhl and served a tour of duty as Mousy Runcible's wife and had a bunch of children with him (all but one of them still living in Balona and avoiding their mother). She had those children before she took up with Ab Crinkle and produced Mitzi, so Mitzi has Balona relatives wherever she turns, Joseph and Kenworth Kuhl only two of the cousins. But Mother Crinkle hardly ever lets one interrupt, or even respond to her errors of fact—one of them, for example, that Mitzi and I have been together for nearly two, not three, years.

The queries keep coming faster and faster, piled one after the other, with hardly a moment for a breath. Poor Soul! Even though she must be in constant pain from the various ills she describes, she keeps any audience pinned with her eyes, which are pale, pale gray-blue, the color of, say, New York harbor in winter, viewed on a foggy day. Mr. D.H. Carp's eyes. Our colonel had eyes like that. Our corpsman, Tom "Feathers" Fethering, informed us that eyes like that meant the person was acquiring, and was soon due for, cataracts.

"But I appreciate you having me stay in your house, y'know, Dan, even with that beast of yours right away stinking up all the furniture; of course it's Mitzi's house and Mitzi's furniture, and you moved in on *her* and of course I'm fully aware of that, old as I am, y'know, I mean, I don't miss much, but even so, I bet it's inconvenient for you having an old lady hanging around coughing and complaining about her aches and pains and making messes in the kitchen and the bathroom and getting in the way all hours of the day and night—but I *could* leave, y'know, sure, I could get my own place and I could move in with one of my other kids, no problem, sure, they'd all have me, sure they would. By the way, you got bad breath today. I should say you got your *usual* dog breath today."

She sniffs twice, pauses, frowns, squints at me. Enjoying conflict as she does, she actually waits for the response. So even though I am sitting across the room I feel obligated to say something, at least about the matter of her living here.

"Well, I stole a shot of Mitzi's special cough medicine this morning, hope it'll do-in this croaking. From sleeping out on the porch. Maybe that's why the offensive breath. I'll try to keep my distance. As for your worry, you're no problem, Mother Crinkle. No problem at all. One enjoys hearing your reminiscences."

I am fibbing. Actually there is a problem. Mother Crinkle is always here and underfoot. Doesn't much use her own room except for night-sleeping. But that's not my main problem. She disliked Lamont immediately, and said so. That's not the problem, either; the real problem that I've already mentioned is that *Mitzi* immediately disliked Lamont, and said so.

Mother Crinkle's problem is she would be deadly lonesome at the Jolly Times Rest Home where Mitzi is eager to deposit her. The old folks there do nothing but sit and watch game show re-runs on the TV or look at the wall. No life for a human being. Too busy in their own withdrawn worlds, the old folks over there would pay no attention to Mother Crinkle. Most human beings need stimulation and responses, or they soon fall apart. Old people especially. A family setting—even a two-person family setting—is best.

But she's mistaken about her other children wanting her. Not one of her children wants her presence. Just the other day one of her older daughters, Lettie Runcible Fring, said she wished her mother would "just die and get it over with." Poor old soul.

"What? What'd you say?"

"You're no problem at all."

"About the baby, Donald, the baby." She got my name right that time.

"The baby? Oh. Well, you'd need to talk to Mitzi about that." There is one other problem, and it is that Mother Crinkle has always hated me. Probably no particullar reason; simply on general principles. I do not take the hatred personally, as Mother Crinkle professes hatred for so many people.

"What? What'd you say? You gotta speak up. You mumble. You always mumble. You oughtta take speech lessons."

Actually, having taught speech and drama to high school students for 20-odd years, I almost always make an effort to speak articulately. I speak now even more articulately: "Mitzi made the decision before we married."

"Well, I don't believe that for one minute, since nobody told *me* that, and Mitzi wut've told me, since a mother has a right to know these things. You mean Mitzi don't want babies, you're nodding 'yes'? How can that be. She never told *me* that. So maybe it's she just dut'n want babies with *you*. She shut've had 'em with that nice Vervex boy...although she wut'n marry him even though he hung around all the time, so I don't know."

Mother Crinkle heaves herself forward so as to be able to get purchase in the carpet with her heavy metal cane, her pale face now suddenly red and puffy with the effort. She begins a soliloquy: "I don't believe for one minute she don't want babies, since there's some evil influence working on my poor Mitzi-girl, mind control probably, and I told her she'd be sorry she married him—not half a man, if that, just look at the scrawny dude—but she went ahead anyways, so that's what you get out of life, just lies and something evil controlling your mind, and no babies."

The *not-half-a-man* hits home. She's on her way toward the kitchen now, still mumbling to herself as she scrapes and stumps her way, dragging her left foot, producing streaks across the dark carpet. Perhaps she has suffered a slight stroke. Perhaps she is faking it. Mumbling loud enough for me to hear, of course, even for Mr. Aflank, the meter reader passing in the side yard, to raise his head and look this way questioningly; he pauses, marches on. He's already turned his flashlight on, for the sun has set.

"That young Vervex boy. Even if his head is kind of pointed, he was the first one wanted to marry her, but no, she held herself out for somebody else, somebody mind-controlling, someone don't like babies. How're you gonna make a decent world when the decent people don't have the babies and the low-lifes have 'em all?"

Sad, frightened, unsatisfied people do cling so to their prejudices; and those prejudices obscure rational thought. Poor soul! I wish I could do something to cheer her up. I could sneak into her room and see if she has a bottle of rubber cement on her desk. No, I can't do that.

Chapter Six

I have bundled myself against the cold and am briskly traversing Seventh Street from our house—Mitzi's house—to Front Street and back, about six blocks in all. I carry a flashlight against the darkness of the streets, keeping it in my coat pocket, navigating porchlight to porchlight. With my excellent vision, and particularly fine night vision, I really need no flashlight. I stop every few meters to listen for possible dog-distress sounds. Balona has many dog sounds, deep *wows,* tinny *yaps,* some muffled, indoor dog-sounds; some backyard dogs, chilly-sounding howls. None distressed. I am resolved to defy Mitzi, build that doghouse—when she has gone on her next rally—even to hiring Binky Swainhammer to cut a hole in the side of the garage.

The air is suddenly redolent of korndog, for King Korndog reigns from the crenelated Kastle Keep at the foot of Seventh Avenue. Having concluded their daily bake, they open their ovens this time of day. The odor is mouth-watering. I like korndogs, possibly from familiarity, as Mitzi serves them to Mother Crinkle, Chum, and me about three times a week, and they have been for years the most-asked-for item at the Balona High cafeteria. I don't dwell on the facts of sausage-making; just enjoy the product without thinking about it. The idea of korndog, at least the *dog* part, reinforces me in my mission.

I never saw many dogs in forward areas. Probably they kept themselves out of the way. Out of harm's way, for too often the few dogs visible might be targets of opportunity to bored or angry army troops (as were water buffalo and the occasional distant civilian), or dinners for hungry villagers. We marines were strictly enjoined not to engage in such activities. For the most part we were compliant, and Americans are said in the media to be dog-lovers. Perhaps so. Once in a while a rear-area unit would have a mutt as a mascot. More often the mascot was a small boy. Neither was official, but the boy was said by its sponsors to be less trouble than a dog, require less supervision, and be more amusing and useful.

Truly, Sergeant Breene's corpse was unrecognizable. In very small pieces. People reared on television don't appreciate the disintegrative effects of high explosives on flesh and bone. "Missing in Action" may very well mean exactly that: *missing.* After the first few sightings of such results, I put the experience out of mind. Not entirely out of mind. In the last year they have all crept back. I had one tour of duty. Nim Chaud did two. Gunny Kevin Black did three. I can only look in wonder at how well and happily those two have survived. Some of us remember their fear. Others confess to having felt nothing but constant boredom or weariness. It is re-markably how different from one another are the expe-riences of survivors. Is Nim really happy? I must put the question to him directly. Nim admits only to head-aches and occasional weeping.

It occurs to me that Lamont might have encountered a mine and have been disintegrated. No, this is Balona. Balona mines affect their victims bloodlessly.

I hear a dog-sound emanating from a garage, and children there, too, shouting along with the dog-sound. Happy dog-sound. Pleasant. I sense myself smiling. As a child I was not allowed pets, so Lamont has affected me as if I were a 10-year-old. I must find him.

The garage. It occurs to me that I have not searched the home premises thoroughly. Perhaps Lamont got into the yard and ate something that poisoned him. Perhaps he is lying in agony under a bush. I hurry home.

Although the Green Giant is in the driveway, I know Mitzi is not yet home because there is no noise coming from the house, usual when Mitzi and Chum are practicing their dance routine or otherwise carrying on.

The only light is from Mother Crinkle's bedroom, where she has her own TV set, electric comforter, radio, microwave oven, portable electric heaters, massage chair, floor lamp, reading lamp, electric devotional niche, fan, and lava lamp—all of them plugged in and frequently running at the same time, a joy for the Pacific Gas and Electric Company and their stockholders. Mother Crinkle must be napping at the moment.

I enter the back porch and turn on the yard lights. The area has bushy plants on the perimeter, but the central grounds are mostly gravel and rocks following the more-or-less artistic plan that Chum volunteered and Mitzi delights in. It is actually a fine place for a backyard party, weather permitting.

The garage, yes. The key to the garage sidedoor hangs on a hook by the back door, so I decide to take a look on the off-chance that somehow Lamont slipped in. Somehow.

As I approach the garage, I hear a low groan coming from within, and a snuffling. I unlock the door and there is Lamont, not rushing toward me in happy greeting.

"I've been waiting all day," he seems to be saying, sitting on his haunches. "I'm thoroughly chilled and quite thirsty."

"How did you get in here?"

"I'll leave that to you to determine." I get a pot from the kitchen and fill it with water from the hosebib next to the back door. Lamont drinks long and deep. He has dehydrated.

How cruel. Mitzi has no consideration for animals. No feeling at all. What a mean-spirited thing to do. Lamont relieves himself on the concrete next to the garage door. He fixes me with an apologetic look as he does his thing.

"You are going to get a nice warm bath. I hope you enjoy water."

I discover that Lamont is a true water dog. Or else he is simply a very complaisant animal beneath the forbidding exterior, for he smiles throughout the experience. It may have been more pleasant because of the lavender bath salts I included in the first bathing, and the lemony softener we used before the final rinse with the shower attachment.

Mitzi's great fluffy yellow towel and her hair dryer set on *warm* completed the exercise.

Afterward, and after Lamont consumes politely a can of the high-class dogfood I bought yesterday at Mr. D.H. Carp's Groceries & Sundries, we settle ourselves comfortably on the couch, I in my maroon robe, Lamont's head in my lap. The warm and generally relaxing ambience pulls me in and I am asleep before I realize it.

She is creaming her beautiful face, a fine soft face that has never required creaming. "There's another one!" she cries, rubbing cream into the corner of her mouth with the tip of her little finger. She's identifying the location of wrinkles, figments of her imagination. I, a person who has better eyesight than anyone in Balona, cannot see a single wrinkle on her face. Why am I in her bedroom?

"And I've got a wrinkle in my neck, right down here in front. That's probably what the suits were all talking about when I was at KDC-TV. That neck wrinkle."

"I have strained my eyes to see your alleged wrinkles and have found not a single one, this from a person who has perfect vision."

51

"You got perfect almost everything, I'm sure, with a certain exception, but you never see anything that means anything, perfect vision or not." Her voice now seems far away.

I suddenly spy that wrinkle after all and decide to have done with it. I pull the pistol from the maroon robe's single pocket where it's been bobbling against the leg. The robe is a gift from a grateful adolescent counselee now adult, the robe's hem presently somewhat tattered. Holding the pistol-gripping hand firmly against the pelvic bone, the way Jack Shaw says he was trained to do, I imagine the trajectory of the bullet proceeding out of the barrel straight into the side of Mitzi's head, abolishing forever worries about wrinkles—and needless discussion of them.

Although I was able to get my hands on a .45 and carried it for almost a year, I never had more than cursory formal pistol training. My officers all insisted we needed to overlearn both the AR-14 and then the AR-16. The sixteen was a tricky beast, given to jamming, maybe fine for rear-echelon honor guards, but not right for the field, a mistake. We much preferred the 14, comparatively clunky but reliable. I must stop thinking about this.

The trigger of the pistol pulls easily, silently. The mechanism makes no noise at all, not even a click. And, surprisingly, the shot itself is soundless, probably because of the silencer. One might compose a note of compliment and mail it off to the manufacturer, much like a letter of reference to a prospective employer, but this from one who has always abhorred violence, gun-produced and otherwise. And the bullet enters into the side of Mitzi's head just above the ear, and she raises her arms like the big-hairdo ladies on the stages at Las Vegas—and falls back out of sight. Is Chum present at the time of the murder? The execution of an animal abuser?

Of course, Lamont and I are then jarred awake by the ruckus the two of them create as they slam the front door and dance in from their run, proceeding as usual directly to the shower.

"My god! Look at this mess!" Mitzi appears over the back of the couch. "All right now! You get that thing out of here right now!" A challenge that Lamont recognizes at once. He lifts his head and displays his fangs, not in a pleasant smile.

I turn my head and address the challenge in a soft but determined tone. "I found him locked in the garage where some heartless person had put him without food or water or company. He stays with me."

"Then you go back to the porch, by god! I will not have that smelly beast sleeping in Daddy's bed."

"I stay, by heaven." I rise and raise my voice. First time ever I raise my voice to her. "You and I may be finished forever, Mitzi. But until the formalities are complete, I stay—and Lamont stays, and we are treated decently. Or else!"

I give her my serious stare, practiced in mirrors since adolescence, the stare Balona teens call a "hard look." I return to the couch; Lamont, also.

"Hey, he got balls after all." This from Chum who is removing her sweat clothes at the bathroom door. Chum has a dark spot in the middle of her chest. It appears to be hair. Naturally I avert my eyes.

Mitzi doesn't ask, "Or else *what?*" as might be expected. She is too much taken aback by my resistance to her will. She is standing quietly, her lips apart, some of the longer blonde hairs caught in the corner of the mouth, no wrinkles visible. It is just as well that she is breathing yet and not actually shot in the head, for she is still a lovely person, despite considerable deficits in merit generally and judgment particularly.

"You promised to love and obey." She is saying this in a small voice, an unfamiliar voice.

"I didn't say I don't love you. I said merely that we are finished as a married couple. I couldn't stand to be married to anyone who abuses animals. Useless husbands, perhaps, but not a helpless animal."

Lamont raises his chin on my lap, closes his eyes.

Mitzi stands there frowning, kneading the wet yellow towel. She drops it to the carpet. "I never abused an animal in my life."

"I found Lamont locked in the garage."

"Did you lock Donald's dog in the garage, Chum?"

"I never locked anybody in your garage."

"Chum wut'n lock even that stinky animal in the garage. Chum's got heart."

Chum sticks her head out of the bathroom again. "You can say that again, so c'mon, let's clean up." She drags Mitzi into the shower. I can hear them carrying on. I wonder if Chum owns a bottle of rubber cement. I am resolved to find out.

Lamont is snoozing, making little satisfied sounds. I examine his paws for signs of damage. No damage. Without a doubt, he has spent the entire lost day in the garage.

Lamont at the animal shelter at first appeared simply another nondescript animal sulking in a far corner of his cage: a medium-size animal, black and dark brown, short hair, one pointed ear failing to stand, large brown eyes looking elsewhere, a big chest and slightly bowed front legs. But he had gray facial markings and expressive eyebrows that helped create the angry countenance.

Unlike the other dogs about to die, Lamont kept his mouth closed. He maintained his detached, standoffish expression. He appeared to be a substantially mature animal, thus far less likely a subject for adoption.

It is widely regarded as true that the dogs we are attracted to somehow resemble us. Or vice versa. I do not see the resemblance in Lamont. Perhaps there are less obvious similar features.

He had been neutered. Perhaps that accounted for his angry countenance. I have discovered that neutered individuals sometimes appear angry; some, of course, make a conscious effort to appear pleasant and to be pleasant. Have I an angry countenance? I have considered my countenance to be mild. Yes, even wimpy.

Lamont's name immediately acquired at the Delta City Animal Shelter was "Old Lemon," shelter volunteer Mrs. Fern Earwick reported to us visitors. The name was a tribute to the dog's effect on potential adoptees rather than to color or parentage. He would growl in his lowest register and lift his upper lip showing those large yellow incisors if anyone came close. He had given even the feeder a grazing bite on the hand.

It was said that yesterday, as shelter association board vice-president Eg Sasifrage stood nearby supposedly safe behind the chain link conversing with Mrs. Earwick, Old Lemon had come out of his corner and had peed with fine accuracy through the fence. Mr. Sasifrage shied away, shook his trouser leg, made a face, probably promised himself to cancel payment on his latest check to the shelter.

As Old Lemon, Lamont had howled all one day and through the night. Mrs. Earwick's gentle persuasions, biscuits, and meaty treats notwithstanding, Old Lemon stayed in his corner. "I have not been at all successful with him," she said.

All this in his first and only week at the shelter. No one at the shelter knew exactly where he had been picked up, for he appeared among six animals brought in by a beer-challenged employee who couldn't remember. "I don't rightly remember if he was from Lathrop or Escalon. Maybe Banta. But from Balona? No, I don't think so. Hell, I don't know. What difference does it make anyways? He's gonna get the Chevy anyways."

I had showed up at the shelter as leader-monitor of a group of youngsters from Tabernacle, those young men and women of high school age who had expressed an interest in veterinary medicine as their possible career. I had hoped to get Doctor Fring to participate, but there was a football game on the tube that afternoon and, besides, it was raining. Doctor Fring encouraged me to "go on ahead, Don. You're much better at that sort of thing than me anyways." I took on the responsibility solo, even though there is some history with two of the youngsters that made me uncomfortable to be with them.

Beauty Jean Dwindle and her younger brother Dirk, Ford Fairlane Kuhl, and Geranium Falz comprised my group—all of them Mitzi's sort of shirt-tail relatives in one degree of relationship or another, and we arrived just at feeding time, noon. There was a lot of noise: barking, growling, hissing, mewing and shouting. The shouting, barking, growling, hissing, and mewing was mostly from Fordy Fairlane. Fordy Fairlane's teachers at Balona High used to mention in their referrals to the counselor (when the counselor was employed at Balona High) that Fordy Fairlane usually shouts; the keeper's shouting was simple showing off, I suppose.

Bootsie's and Gerry's behavior was exemplary, except that Bootsie insisted on holding one of my hands wetly, complaining of fear of "wild animals." Gerry kept watching her hand-holding behavior, with me trying to extricate myself.

Dirk, a needful child, tightly grasped my other hand. Dirk's grip is also moist. I tried to get him to release me, with no success. Gerry watched and smirked. I said several times, "You need to go with Fordy, Dirk. Go look at the puppies there." Dirk would not let go.

Dirk is susceptible to colds, chills, and various frights. Dirk's mother refers to the young man as "Dirky," a name modified to "Turkey" by Dirk's classmates who often shout that modification at him repeatedly, producing the aforementioned tears. I should point out that Dirk is 14-years-old, not at all a tiny child, though his nose needs frequent wiping and he seems unaware of the need. Like Bootsie, Dirk has a long neck and a prominent forehead. An unkind person would consider the name "Turkey" somewhat reminiscent, if not actually descriptive.

"Bootsie, please go with Gerry and check out the kittens there, will you?" Bootsie would not, expressing fears that she might slip on the wet concrete or be attacked by a vulture. She grasped my hand more tightly. I groaned inwardly; Gerry smirked and walked off by herself.

The keeper, a tiny man in a red beanie and a nose to match, appeared grim, not used to visitors in groups. He frowned at Fordy Fairlane especially, and was not responsive to questions, seemed unwilling to comment on the animals, on his own duties, on how one is educated to become a shelter keeper, et cetera.

We—the youngsters and I—were saddened at the sight of so many animals waiting. Mrs. Earwick took on the responsibility of showing us the layout of the shelter. Mrs. Earwick also explained at length the process by which the keeper herds or flings unadopted victims weekly into a sort of tank, then stuffs one end of a hose into the tank and the other into the exhaust pipe of his old Chevrolet pickup, a polluting vehicle.

"It takes them about two hours to die, barking and mewling and howling. It's awful," Mrs. Fern Earwick reported, bobbing her head in sympathy.

"Only about a quarter of a tank gasoline," added the keeper. "Still good mileage on that old baby."

"And then they shovel those poor bodies into a truck and take them for rendering over at Fruitstand."

Mrs. Earwick then described the rendering process in some detail. Fordy looked interested. Bootsie and Dirk clutched my hands spasmodically, and Gerry paled, became thoughtful, ceased chattering.

"We're coming to the end of the week again," Mrs. Earwick mentioned. An ominous mention.

Before the explanations, Bootsie and Gerry had been gasping with admiration over certain of the cats and dogs, kittens and puppies who seemed to be starved for attention. The young women then began to weep, and Fordy Fairlane asked where the toilet was, left noisily for that facility. I released myself from Dirk's and Bootsie's grasp, hunkered down next to the cage where Old Lemon sulked. To support my posture I clutched the chain link cage wall, watching the animals and the visitors. I was surprised to feel warmth on my fingers.

"You better getcher fingers outta there, Squire. He'll gnaw 'em right off, that Old Lemon will."

The warmth I felt was Old Lemon's tongue. He sat back and examined me. We examined each other. He raised his eyebrows and smiled. "Oh, my," I said, quite taken aback. "I can't possibly adopt you, old boy. My wife would have a fit, you know, not to speak of my mother-in-law."

Old Lemon *groaned*, marched back to his corner and sat, his back turned to me. The message was powerful.

"Does this dog have all the shots he needs?"

Mrs. Fern Earwick responded officially, "All our animals must have their shots, y'know, before we can let them go with an adoptor. We administer all the necessary shots right here on premises. And they must be spayed or neutered." She squinched her eyes. "The animals, I mean!"

Old Lemon turned only his head from the corner, looked back at me, eyebrows raised again.

"I might be able to take him for a while, on trial y'know."

"Oh, no. You have to decide right now, once and for all. We can't have animals coming and going like that."

Old Lemon returned, sat looking at Mrs. Earwick and me. His gaze reminded me suddenly of the intense long brown stare of Lance Corporal Asher Bernstein watching for jungle dangers. Bootsie pulled on my fingers and Gerry pleaded for Old Lemon's life. Even Fordy Fairlane observed that it looked like a "clean dog" to him. The keeper almost smiled. Old Lemon almost smiled, eyebrows up.

"Okay. Let's do it." And the keeper brought Old Lemon—now Lamont—out at once for his shots and for the trip home. He sat in the front seat on the way back to Balona, between Fordy Fairlane and me, Fordy driving, of course. We secured Lamont with the seatbelt. All the way back he leaned his weight against me, looking at my face occasionally and smiling. Fordy whistled "Go Baloney." Gerry looked out the window at the rain. Bootsie and Dirk both cried.

"Why are you crying, Beauty Jean?"

"I'm thinking about all the dead animals in the world."

"Ah, well. There are lots of little baby animals, too, growing up healthy and well taken-care-of."

"I'm not thinking about them. I'm thinking about the dead ones."

"Ah, well. And why are you crying, Dirk?"

"I'm hungry."

I thought about Bootsie's and Dirk's concerns and about Lamont's intense gaze and about 30-years-dead "Ace" Bernstein and the transmigration of souls and whether that belief might have some validity in this Twenty-first Century. I should have died 30 years ago. I wondered if I were destined to die soon.

All that transpired just a few days ago. I am still wondering.

⚜

Chapter Seven

I sit on the couch with my friend Lamont, a warm, clean-smelling, fully hydrated dog who is napping with his head on my lap. Mother Crinkle is also napping, in her own room for a change. Mitzi is with Chum traversing Chaud County roads, practicing their rally skills in the Green Giant. I consider my retirement from education and how it came about. Was it planned? It was a remarkable surprise.

Picture my office environment in the last week of school.

Miss Candy Wishingfor's desk is in the middle of the main office at Balona High. Blonde Goddess Candy is secretary to both the principal and the superintendent. Mr. Abel Croon's spartan office lies just behind her. Superintendent Doctor Thrust's less spartan office is off to the side.

My office was more of an unnoticeable cubicle tacked into a corner. The cubicle was never very satisfactory for counseling, for the door was sliding glass and there was no ducting for heating, ventilating, and cooling. If one slid the door closed because a student was relating something confidential, both counselor and counselee were soon gasping for fresh air. And there was room for but two chairs besides mine, so if one wished to confer privately with both parents and a child, one would have to reserve a classroom after school. Most of the old-line faculty discourage such use of their rooms.

I was sitting in my office very late that afternoon last May, doing the paperwork that any solitary high school counselor necessarily must address if he cares about maintaining both sanity and decent records. Miss Candy had taken another "few minutes—be right back" to drive up First Avenue to Doctor Fring's place, to check on the recovery of her sick poodle, Manon. She had put her incoming calls on the machine. I had the sliding glass cracked open and my desk lamp off to try to keep the temperature down. Candy's perfume—sweet, new, unfamiliar—hung in the air.

I recognized the voices of the three persons who had come in the office and seated themselves along the wall. I have previously mentioned Beauty Jean Dwindle who was now weeping. Not unusual for Bootsie, of course. During the year she had spent a good deal of class time in my office weeping and complaining about her mother. As one subject to spells of weeping myself, I did not object to the weeping, but I tried to derail the complaining and help Bootsie re-focus into productive uses of her energy. I had recognized the complaints as representing what some of my textbooks refer to as "adolescent angst."

"Anyways, I know he loves me, too." This from Bootsie.

"He's an old man. He's certainly not interested in a young girl who don't even hang up her clothes or make her bed." This from Amy Beach Langsam Dwindle, Bootsie's mother.

Bootsie's father is Junior Dwindle. Junior is Balona High's woodshop teacher. His voice is unique, kind of like a band-saw under stress. In the circumstances he has lowered it to a raspy whisper. "I don't wanna hear no more of that stuff about love. And I'm not gonna go sit in there and listen to it, either. So I'll see you to house later. You'll thank me if I don't tan your hide."

Junior departs muttering. Bootsie weeps.

Bootsie must be referring to a new love. She has a new one about once a month. Gender is immaterial with Bootsie, recent love-objects having been both Patella Sackworth and Sammy Jack Sly in tandem. And genus is sometimes inconsequential, as Bootsie recently confessed having passionate feelings about Sal Shaw's handsome horse. Bootsie's hormones are bubbling, so an "old man" is not out of the question.

There is mumbling from Mr. Croon's doorway, and Bootsie and her mother disappear into the principal's office. The door is closed but I can hear wailing within. Perhaps Mr. Croon himself is the love object despite his 40-something age, his egg-shaped pink head, and his hunched posture.

I noticed that Dirk was not accompanying his mother today. Dirk, the slow and needful child mentioned previously, is completing his freshman year. The striking family resemblance shared by Bootsie, Dirk, Amy, and Junior is the "strong" rounded forehead beneath which the eyes seem almost to disappear. Dirk's red hair is a family anomaly.

Amy Dwindle resembles her husband remarkably, is described as "generously proportioned." She has a high voice and sings in Tabernacle's choir..

I thought no more about the Dwindles, considering instead how I was going to rearrange my methods in order to be able to serve more students more efficiently next year. That very night was the meeting of the school board that was to change this phase of my life. Candy had not returned. I gathered up my things and went home for a dish of instant noodles before the meeting.

What was it my friend Abel Croon said before that same meeting of the school board during which counseling was abolished? He invited me to be sure to attend. "You are scheduled for a surprise," he mentioned.

I was surprised.

"I will tell you, ladies and gentlemen of the Board," (this is the way Abel Croon always addresses any group, as ladies and gentlemen, although there were at that time no ladies on the board). "Before I say anything about our budget problem and about our ingenuous and creative solution here at Balona High School, I want you to know that Donald Keyshot is a fine worker. He is always here early and late. He is always ready to help a student out, even to the point of getting them off and sending them back to class unpunished when they've really been sent to the office to see the principal for discipline." Abel Croon chuckled and squinched his eyes in good humor. There were mutters from a few of the teachers, pro and con, I suppose.

I recall that all five board members turned their eyes on me when Abel said that. Abel was very nervous, moving from one foot to the other and wringing his hands, and one could excuse him because of that, although the way it *sounded* was that I, Donald Keyshot, worked hard to undermine the influence and importance and authority of the principal.

But that was not what he meant, I'm sure.

Then he said something like, "Mr. Keyshot has been real close to the school and the community, not to speak of the students, some of them especially, I have heard."

Mr. Sam Joe Sly, heir to and operator of the King Korndog plant and a rare visitor to school board meetings, then made a loud remark from the audience. Mr. Sly is courageously running again for State Assembly already, having only recently been thrashed at the polls.

"We hear Mr. Keyshot likes some of the students specially good."

There was laughter. I laughed and nodded my head in agreement with this truth.

I *do* like some of the youngsters especially. I don't like a few of them, but I try not to let on about that.

And then Abel Croon asked me to step forward, and he presented me with a certificate, signed by him, revealing that he, Abel Croon, certified Donald Keyshot as a Valued Educator, dated this date, et cetera. There was applause and Abel showed all of his front teeth in a nice smile, shook my hand. I sat down thinking, "That was nice. I wonder if I should hint to Abel that he needs to see his dentist." Well, it's pleasant to be recognized, however clumsily it's done. I read the certificate again and noticed that it was signed also by Doctor Thrust and the Chaud County Superintendent of Schools. And by Mr. Kenworth Burnross, Esquire, attorney for the board. Official.

"Anyways," continued Abel Croon, "we been looking over the budget and the fact that we're gonna have less students next year. We figure—our business manager Mr. Zerky Vervex and Doctor Thrust and me—we figure that we'll just about run out of money pretty soon unless we do something about it, and there's only one pot of money, so we're recommending that we cut out the counselor job and so then, even so, we can give the faculty a small raise which they been griping for. So this is actually a real good time for that fine educator Mr. Donald Keyshot to take his early retirement. So let's hear a nice round of applause for Mr. Don Keyshot." There was applause from the faculty members in the audience, led by Audrey Frackle.

The meeting was then brief and there was coffee cake and coffee afterwards, and people stood around and chatted for a few minutes as they usually do after board meetings. Sid Weiner came up to me and congratulated me on "getting out of this rat-race."

Some parents of former students shook my hand, confessed surprise that I was leaving. I smiled, nodded, agreeing.

I had a piece of coffee cake and went home and told Mitzi I was retiring.

"How come? You're not old enough to qualify for retirement."

"They say there's a special way you can retire early, so that's what I'll do."

She sniffed. "I guess you're going to hang around the house and mope."

"I hope to help out Pastor Nim and I'm going into private practice, too, soon as my license comes through. And we'll still have my disability check coming each month along with the retirement money."

"Big deal. You might have talked it over with me before you made a big decision like this. I mean after all I'm not re-employed yet, and my severance is gonna last only so long."

"I didn't know it was going to happen. My retirement."

"What? *What?*"

Then Mitzi and I had a sort of discussion, which was joined by Chum who happens usually to be present when we have serious discussions.

"Somebody accused him of buggering little Turkey Dwindle. Dit'n you hear? That's how come they're retiring him."

"What?" Both Mitzi and I shouted at Chum's atypically quiet observation.

"Yeh. It's all over town. That's how come Don is retiring. Everybody knows that. Don't that take the cake?" She laughs, shaking her head. "The other story is that there's something going on with you and Bootsie."

"Turkey *and* Bootsie, I mean Dirky, uh Dirk? That's nonsense. They're both needful kids who hang onto me. I can't seem to...."

"Well, don't blame me for telling you what's all over Balona. Don't blame the messenger, like Shakespeare always says. Anyways, lots of people don't believe it. They know Junior and Amy Dwindle and their weird kids and they figure Don is just, well, Don. In the way. y'know?"

"Those kids're my cousins or something. Maybe I can talk to them. To the school board, I mean."

"About what, Mits? This is Balona. Remember what happened to Kork the year he was principal? Remember what happened to Mr. Hill about the typing class? Remember what happened to Superintendent Lucia Roturier-Lutz about the missing money? Hey, Mits, remember what's happened to *you!* It's a done deal. Let's just help Don do his new thing."

Nim hinted at it. Mr. D.H. Carp suggested it. Joseph Kuhl came out and said it. In effect I have been dismissed from my counseling job at Balona High School. The retirement was only the formality of it, one of the outcomes. It was not my choice, as I am short a number of years to qualify for full retirement and the benefits that go with it. I must make a success of my private counseling in order to help provide for my wife with a decent family income. I have not faced up to all the facts.

I wonder if Mrs. Bellona Shaw has a bottle of glue or paste on her desk. Sure, I bet she does.

Chapter Eight

I am sitting in my chair, Lamont lying beside, amazingly asleep, occasionally twitching. The room is warm and noisy.

"I'm hungry for pizza." Chum's vowels are easily heard even over Aretha Franklin's high notes.

"Chum, turn that damn thing down. Don, go get us some pizza. Plenty anchovies and linguiça, too. And some Valley Brew." Mitzi is in her Drill Instructor mode.

"Don can't get us pizza. Don dut'n drive."

"Jess wants to try out the Giant. So here, Jess, you take my keys and my husband, and off with you to Mello Fello."

"Okay, Mitzi." Jess Pleroma quite banters my wife's name. Although I have never seen him up close, he reminds me of the actor Sylvester Stallone—without Stallone's lips, eyes, or muscles. Just something about his attitude. And maybe the curly hair and the suggestion of concealed tattoos. He sneaks a look at me. "Okay, Wimpy! We're, y'know, off!"

Jess has now on record directly referred to me as "Wimpy." Possibly resulting from my never answering back, my meek facial expression, my half-smile whenever he makes what he probably thinks is an insulting remark. I am trying the tactic Nim is so fond of: *A soft answer turneth away wrath.* Maybe a soft expression will turneth away Jess's insulting demeanor. Doesn't matter either way.

I am somehow keenly aware that the leather seat is cold. I wonder where Lamont is. Jess has nothing to say as he grinds the Giant's starter over Aretha's wails. I almost expect Mitzi to run out onto the front porch expostulating. No, she is otherwise occupied.

Jess flashes me a sidelong glance occasionally as we vroom up Seventh Avenue to Front Street. I do believe Mitzi may have had Hanky Fring pack the Giant's muffler with steel wool for it is making a fine new noise, a bit like our kitchen blender, remarkably similar to what I have been told my own snoring sounds like. Jess gears down with lots of show and slows considerably as we approach Cod's stoplight, peculiarly and effectively placed mid-block in front of the constable's office. Evidently Cod is at Frank's having a second supper, for we don't have to try to figure out Cod's thumb-play as he manipulates the green-yellow-red light to the detriment of foreign travelers caught on Balona's main street. The light stays green. I've never met Jess Pleroma face to face. This is very real.

We turn onto Airport Way. My stomach growls. I, too, like pizza and I had no lunch today. The radio still plays Aretha. "I guess the gears, like, y'know, confuse you, huh, Wimpy?"

Jess is laughing at my alleged incompetence. "I thought everybody who's, like, anybody, knows how to drive. I mean, it's like, y'know, a thing guys do. Drive, like."

"Is that a fact." I am being non-combative. What would be the point of "winning" here?

"That's a fact all right. Guys who don't know how to drive are, like, y'know, maybe not much of a guy."

"That could be true."

"Mitzi's quite a chick."

I chuckle, prepared to be tolerant. "Don't let her hear you refer to her as a 'chick.'"

"Oh, yeh? I could probably refer to her, like, y'know, anything I want. She likes me."

"She does have some odd likes and dislikes."

He looks at me again, not sure whether that was a comment or a challenge. He is chewing, loudly—over the Giant's roar and Aretha's whine—and popping gum that smells like cinnamon over the exhaust. The smell of cinnamon is very real. Jess turns the Giant into Mello Fello's crunchy gravel parking lot. "You're paying, right? Because, y'know, like I don't got even a dollar in change. So you better, like, break out the old wallet."

"You might secure the vehicle, Jess, since it's after dark and people around here after dark are fond of borrowing cars." Jess is said to know all about borrowing cars.

"'Secure the vehicle...' Shee-it! How you gonna, like, lock it secure when it's got a canvas top and anybody with a blade..."

"I meant take the keys out of the ignition, thus discouraging the vagrant opportunist."

"Jesus," he exclaims. "You talk like a goddam old lady. No wonder Mitzi can't stand you. What a wimp!"

I smile, waiting my opportunity. My neck is stiff. I try to move it but it is stuck in position.

Mello Fello is crowded tonight. A couple of ex-colleagues from Balona High are drinking beer with their pizza in a corner. I wave at Elvis Drumhandler, history, and Sid Weiner, ag. I wonder if they've still got poor Sid trying to teach French. The teachers return the greeting. Coach Kork Sporlodden is standing at the head of the line, looks back, smiles. The Ordways, Mark and Jack and Jack's little sister are back in the crowd, eating already at a table with Ms Penny Preene from Tabernacle and her daughter Claire. They, too, wave.

Everyone is so nice, even considering the circumstances of my retirement.

There are also some rough people at the end of the line, jostling folks. I can hear one talking dirty over the crowd noise.

This is very realistic.

Jess Pleroma goes over to the Ordways and stands there, making important-guy faces for Claire Preene and Mark Ordway, Jess's brother-in-law. Step-brother-in-law. Where have I witnessed this scene played out before? Perhaps at Mello Fello. The odor of pizzas baking is strong, appetizing. I am sleepy from the warmth of the place and the good feeling.

A large smelly T-shirted man pushes in line in front of me. He gives me a hard look. "You don't got an objection, right, Grandpa?" He leans backward, leers at me. I wonder if he's been drinking. "I know you. You're the queer got fired from Big Baloney. The guy plays with little boys." He confirms this with his friend, a smaller version of himself, and they both guffaw. "So you don't mind me taking your place in line, I guess."

I can feel my blood rising, my face flaming. I answer sharply. "No problem, long as I'm ahead of you when they ask for my order." I show my teeth at these bullies who happen to be my new clients, Junior Trilbend and his friend Bobby R. Langsam.

"You hear this old guy? This white-hair queer? He got no problem long as he's ahead of me at the counter. You goddam fag, I'm gonna run you outta this place."

He begins to make the attempt and my patience crumbles. He gets two stiff fingers to the throat, then the wedge to the solar plexus, then as he stands gagging, I apply what the Japanese call *tai otoshi,* the body drop. Then comes the problem. I cannot stop myself. The rage comes and I begin kicking him as he lies. There is something familiar to this action, this berserker violence. Where have I performed it before? It feels so good.

But I'm wearing moccasins and neglect the curl-back of the toes one doesn't require when wearing combat boots, so that is when I see that his cheekbone has opened, I also realize my foot is hurting. My crotch aches. As expected, Bobby R. Langsam has backed away and is standing open-mouthed, not believing that his County-appointed wimp therapist would attack a client. Even counter-attack a client.

It's Mark Ordway who leads me away from my attacker-victim, sits me down in the suddenly quiet room, pats me on the shoulder. "What can Mr. Runcible get you, Mr. Keyshot?" He's referring to the owner, who's standing there, rubbing his hands, smiling. Nobody seems to be eating and drinking; everybody is watching. Nobody is calling me a bugger. Is this the way I can be rehabilitated in the eyes of the public?

Owner Mr. Orris Runcible says, "Sir, that Junior Trilbend and his friend are no-goods. I'm glad you told him off like you did."

Junior Trilbend's smaller friend was leading Junior out of the building. Junior was not objecting. I look around. Jess is missing. I hope he hasn't run off with the Giant. Mitzi would be angry. I think Mitzi would be very angry. I order enough pizza and beer for the three of us and Mother Crinkle and sit with the Ordways until the order is ready. We talk about the quality of pizza here as opposed to Delta City's providers. Everybody is very polite, but they keep looking at me, undoubtedly cotrasting my constant message in my Tabernacle group-counseling sessions ("reconciliation") with my behavior tonight. But no one asks any questioins. They just look. It's anyway a more temperate, even admiring, look than I've been getting since that last board meeting at school. It's almost *respectful.*

How is it that people can view as reprehensible the acts of charity that tipped the scales of my retirement, and see a violent act like mine tonight as respectable? Mark gives me a ride home in his Plymouth.

"Don! Don! Wake up."

It's Chum's rough voice shouting in my ear. "Pizza's out of the oven, sitting on the table. We made up some

Orange Juliuses, too. We been waiting for you. Whas-samatta you? You sick? You been snoring again when you weren't making noises like a puppy. I think maybe he's sick, Mits."

Mitzi cries, "He's not sick. He's just asleep. He's always sleeping. Are you still asleep? For heavensakes wake up. He sleeps all day, then he walks around all night, complaining he's got insomnia and headaches."

It was so real. I trip over Lamont on the way to the table. At least Mitzi is not harping on Lamont in the house tonight. It's bitter cold outside, I'm sure. That bone-chilling delta fog again. "Is Jess here?" I ask this of the table generally.

Mitzi looks at Chum; Chum looks at Mitzi. "You mean Jess Pleroma, of course, the boy wants to buy my Giant. Why should he be here? I'm not gonna sell him my Giant. Me and Chum got a rally day after tomorrow. You think I would sell my Giant before an important rally? He dut'n think much of my sense. Well, I don't think much of his sense."

They converse with their mouths full, Balona style, waiting until their mouths are full to begin any sentence, each speaking as the other speaks, woman style, the way it's done on the TV talk shows. Amazing that they can understand each other.

Mother Crinkle, staring at the tablecloth, intrudes: "Dut'n the mother get any?" She whines this in a low voice, repeats it.

"I'll serve you, Mother Crinkle." I begin to make the effort.

"I want Mitzi to serve me. You serve me, Miriam." Mother Crinkle pounds the tip of her cane into the floor several times like a pile driver. Remarkable the sound she can get with that cane, even rubber-tipped.

"I'm eating, Mother. Can't you see I've got both hands full here? Just lean over and grab a piece. Won't break your back just to lean over."

"I don't want any pizza. Sticks to my dentures, burns your lips. Gives wrinkles."

Mitzi pauses, pizza half-way to her mouth. "That's just about enough of that, Mother, or you can just go back to your room and use your own damn microwave for a change."

Mother Crinkle heaves herself to her feet and humps herself away from the table, toward her room. She doesn't appear to be as handicapped using her cane as when she uses her walker. "I know when I'm not wanted. You don't have to coldcock me with a shovel."

"Oh, for godsakes!"

"Hey, Mits, let her go. She's gonna go watch her gameshow, and she's too fat anyways. Do her good to lay off the pizza. Gimme another piece there, long as Mama don't want it." Chum plays lacrosse, puts the shot, and is taking kick-boxing lessons. She doesn't seem to mind the off-the-shoulder hard look she's getting from retreating Mother Crinkle. Or am I the target of that look?

While I'm washing down pizza with my Valley Brew I'm wondering again if Mother Crinkle has glue or paste or rubber cement on her table in there. And if maybe my clients Junior Trilbend and Bobby R. Langsam are competent enough to compose cut-and-paste hate mail.

✤
Chapter Nine

At least Lamont seems to be accepted. No, better say *tolerated.* They gossip in front of me, as if Lamont and I weren't present. Occasionally one or the other will turn and ask me to confirm a fact, spell a word, assay a solution. But usually it's Mitzi and Chum, a twosome complete.

"You maybe oughtta watch your husband here, about Candy. Candy's got the hots for him, I hear. Talks about him all the time. About missing him in the office there. Driving Mr. Croon crazy. She's always talking about Don here. But anyways, if I was so inclined, I'd go after Nim Chaud."

"Who said about Candy hot for Don? Where'd you hear that?" It's remarkable how a woman can be immediately jealous of another woman merely from having heard unsupportable idle gossip. "Who said?"

"I don't know who said. I just hear Candy sighing about Don every once in a while, and notice how Mr. Croon frowns when she sighs like that. That's all."

"Well, Don's not interested in Candy Wishingfor. The idear. Why would he be interested in a girl young enough to be his daughter? He might as well actually be interested in that little Bootsie thing. Don, you hear what we've been talking about?"

I feign nap behavior.

"He's sleeping again. See, I told you he's always like that. Candy wut'n be interested in Don, for heavensakes."

"You never know." Chum is teasing. Mitzi is serious.

Mitzi pursues the argument, but changes subjects. "What about Jess, then? You'd go after Jess, too, if you were so inclined, like you said?"

"Well, he's pretty enough, but there's a good deal missing there. You know."

"Well, I *don't* know, as a matter of fact. Maybe I'll find out. He keeps stalking me and asting me do I want to sell the Giant."

"Jess Pleroma's never bought a car in his life. He gets 'em free from stupid women. You gonna give him your Giant?"

"You're not suggesting I'm stupid by any chance?"

"Depends on how you act around Jess. You gonna take a side-trail with Jess Pleroma now, the way you said you did with Blip Wufser?"

"Looks to me like maybe little Jess's got it all. Just dut'n show."

"All including that stupid tattoo."

"He used to have 'em on both hands. One saying *love,* the other *hate.* I think only *love* is left. Got scars on the other hand. Imaginative guy."

"Really classy, Mits. A kid got kicked out of Big Baloney, for petesakes, and been in jail how many times! And also young enough to be somebody's son."

"Aw, I'm just kidding. C'mon in the kitchen. I got something to show you for a minute or so."

Mitzi pulls Chum out of her chair and they repair to the kitchen whence emanate some snuffling noises and muffled exclamations, but no speech. At least they have the decency to do their making-out in semi-private. In its way, their love-making is stimulating. I have a pain in my crotch, dig in my shirt for the requisite aspirin.

She would never let me express my love physically, even to hugging and kissing. "I hate that stuff. Daddy was always grabbing me, rubbing my privates and hugging and breathing and slobbering."

Denied and in love, I once asked her, "What about Chum touching and hugging and kissing and slobbering?"

"That's different. You're supposed to be a psychologist. You figure out why it's different."

"But you think about men."

"I think about men the way you think about philosophers and music."

"And Blip?"

"Blip? Well, uh, Blip and the others just sort of happened. I don't think about them any more. Just colleagues being friendly."

Occasionally we will accidentally encounter KDC-TV ace newscaster Blip Wufser in Delta City. "Hi, Blip!" Mitzi will cry in a voice higher than usual.

"Bow-wow!" Blip will respond mysteriously, and pant, his tongue extended suggestively. They seem to have had something going.

I put on my coat and leave the house. Interesting how Mitzi is outraged at the idea of another woman finding me attractive. Maybe I should tell her that Bellona Shaw said I was very handsome, in my way. Maybe I ought to take only one shot a week, instead of two, save Balona women from insanity.

I find it salubrious to go to my new private office sometimes several times a day, necessary or not, to straighten up, get ready for whatever clients may show. I wipe possible motes of dust off my new gold-on-black plastic sign on the building entrance at the foot of the stairs. The plaque reads like the label on a pair of English gloves or Scotch whiskey:

Donald Keyshot MFCC
by Appointment

The office is of course still tidy. I put on a CD, lie back in my chair and relax to Henry Mancini oldies.

The phone rings as at a distance.

"Your wife Mitzi Crinkle? Used to be that big TV personality? Well, same one seems to be dead over here," the phone-caller had cried. "I think it's your wife, only it's hard to tell with the way her head hit first, and the blood. So maybe you need to come on over to the gate of the dump, and there she'll be, you know, so's you can identify her. They haven't moved her yet."

"Who is calling, please?" I try always to be courteous, whatever the circumstances.

"Uh, well, it's Frank Floom if ya wanna know. So, I'm sorry for your trouble, Mr. Keyshot, but you better get over there right away. It's gotta be done."

"She must've fell off from up there." This from Constable Cod Gosling, a monstrously obese, goodhearted man still in his forties but appearing much older. "Right on her head, too. Maybe took a dive, I guess."

Here she lies on the asphalt approach to the East Bridge that spans the Yulumne River. I have at once hastened to the this place next to the Balona Dump, a noisome, noxious place, winter, summer or fall.

Flies are gathering in the shiny black mess around her head. It is as the constable has said. Death takes us unawares as we ourselves race unknowing to greet the Dark Angel. Perhaps it was the worry again about the wrinkle. Terrible, but from a selfish point of view at least I'm finally done with that particular worry.

I am brought back to complete wakefulness in my chair by the jarring of the telephone's bell, not a gentle electronic wail, but an insistent mechanical jangle. It is Mitzi, of course, not lying beneath the overpass dead, but alive and shouting at me over the telephone "When you coming home, Don? I been waiting dinner here for you, and I gotta go out tonight to see, uh, to see somebody, y'know. So, I'll leave the plate on the turntable in the microwave and you can zap it when you feel like it. Mother's already been fed, so you don't need to disturb her."

I don't much feel hungry so I meander down the noisy stairs and walk home in the usual direction, the long way around: north on Front Street to First Avenue, east on First to King Way, then south on King Way and west briefly on Seventh to the place I call home.

But I stop off at Tabernacle. Pastor Nim's office light is on. The Boysenberry bushes that Nim has planted around the Tabernacle campus are glossy green in spring and summer, produce the largest, juiciest berries, beloved of squirrels, birds, and courageous tough-handed parishoners. But in autumn the bushes turn sere. The green leaves drop. Only bare brown stems remain. Life is like that. That *is* life: green leaves, then brown stems and thorns. Have I mentioned that? But there is also hope, says Nim.

He has already changed the legend in his outdoor bulletin board: *When many cares fill my mind, your consolations cheer my soul. Psalm 94*

Pastor Nim proclaims the beauty of all life, in stasis or in bloom. He planted the berry bushes for a reason, perhaps several different, even conflicting, reasons. He is a good man. Misguided about a good many practical things, but a solid friend, especially to those who feel the pain of the world keenly.

I enter without knocking, take a seat in his "victim's chair," as he calls it, a nice padded-leather seat with a high back and wood arms.

"I should apologize for intruding like this."

"You're not intruding, Don. *Semper Fi*, Keyhole." He looks straight at me, smiles. "Can I be any help, old friend?"

I avoid looking at the pile of papers he's been examining, evidence of serious work I have interrupted. "It doesn't necessarily signify that one is crying for help because one chooses to drop in and chat with a friend."

"Not necessarily. Of course."

"About our common experiences. People might look at me and say, 'You were a marine? You don't look like a marine.' What do I say to that?"

"I sometimes get the same thing. I was under the impression you don't volunteer information about your service."

"They also imply, 'You're too wimpy to be a marine.' They say, 'You're too skinny and sad-looking to be a marine.'"

"I get, 'You're too tall to be a marine. They wouldn't take you.' I say, 'Nevertheless, there I was.' You could say the same. Anyway, we both know it makes no difference now. It was a long time ago and we have our history. And they are commenting probably out of sincere interest."

"One could have unresolved worries, not necessarily major."

"Yes. Folks often have."

"One could worry about one's wife and yet not be seriously concerned. That is, one could treat oneself to unnecessary worries."

"Treat oneself."

"A manner of speaking. Have you ever read Saint Augustine? Imagine, my asking *you* this question. Of course you have."

"Well, I confess: only *Confessions.*"

"Great work." We sit there in silence for some minutes, I thinking, he waiting. "Well, one's corporeal presence requires sustenance." I prepare to rise, leaning forward in the chair as if to leave, almost laughing aloud at how stuffy and phony my words sound.

"Yes. Sure. Come on back, Don, whenever you feel the need. Your second office is right next door, after all. And you know how I appreciate your sharing your expertise with the congregation. The youngsters often remark on your patience and your kindness."

"They sometimes make up stories."

"Ah. I believe it's the adults who make up the most hurtful stories. In Balona they seem to do it for fun. I've done more than one sermon on that problem: *the poison of asps is under their lips.*" Nim rubs his beard, wags his head.

"It's no fun when you're the innocent target."

"Well, it's water under the bridge, Don. Try to put it out of your head. Stash it away with your 'wimp-note.' You're not still hanging on to that, are you?"

"Got it right here." I pat my shirt pocket.

"Handsome shirt."

"Gift from Mitzi. No special reason. Just a gift. We give each other gifts like that, for no reason." Why am I lying to this good man? I'm the giver. Mitzi's the receiver of offerings.

"Nice to have a relationship like that."

"Well... I always come to this office in friendship."

"I welcome that friendship. Treasure it, in fact."

"Bless you."

"I sincerely hope so." He laughs and slaps his knee in good humor. His teeth are clean. His breath is sweet. He is a pure man.

"I am having fantasies." Shall I reveal the depths of my degrading images?

"Join the crowd!"

"About violent and unpleasant things."

"Still flashbacks."

"Oh, those, too. But the flashbacks have diminished greatly over the years. And the weeping."

"Then you're one of us luckier ones."

"They're now almost peripheral, the passing moments—the flashbacks, not the dreams and the fantasies. The flashbacks are about the stuff that happened years and years ago, right?

"And I didn't do anything over there that I need to be especially ashamed of, right? I mean, I did my job.

Nothing to be really, *particularly* ashamed of. Sort of ashamed, maybe, right? But these fantasies now. No, these are *meditations.*"

"Well, good for you, Don. I wish I could forget some of the things I did over there. Some I had to do to save my life. Other things I chose. The choices still tell me something about myself. Something not quite worthy. Even after all these years those choices haunt me."

I can't imagine Nimitz Chaud doing anything untoward, even as a marine in combat. He was a polite-as-possible marine. I always saw him that way. This confession is strange. Perhaps it was my mentioning Saint Augustine.

The flash returns without warning, as I am sitting in Nim's office readying myself to rise and leave for the microwaved nourishment that awaits me on Seventh Avenue.

This is not the way it's supposed to be. It's supposed to hit—and usually does—when there's nothing else on your mind, when maybe there's no one around. Not this time. This is different. Nim's spotless office even smells suddenly moldy.

In the hootch I at once catch sight of another marine already there, a man also evidently tall and thin, very thin. An odd thing: the marine has the same brown eyes as my own. His eyes look troubled. The guy takes off his fatigue hat, his "floppy," and runs his fingers through the fuzz; familiar, too, the scrubby thatch of uncombable fur on top of the head. Purple half-moons under the eyes now, as if from lack of sleep for days.

He looks so familiar, thin hands with long fingers and scabs on the knuckles, from old scratches probably, the same kind I got scrabbling through the brush; dirty fingernails. Older than your typical marine, he looks like he might be a teacher in civilian life, but I can't identify him.

It's obvious that he is deeply angry.

A young Asian man dressed in the usual loose black sits at the rough table. He lifts his upper lip, as if in a sneer or is it a smile?

The marine replaces his cover, looks me straight in the face, and puts a finger to his lips in that universal gesture signaling silence. The marine draws his .45, raises the heavy pistol, and shoots the young man sitting at the table. The slug enters between the eyes. The sound is brief, like a handclap inside a box, not like a .45 at all.

Before the Corps, I had always thought that when you shot someone in the head from close up, the victim would be blown backwards by the force of the slug. That's what victims always did in the movies. "Blown away," they said. This young man leaning with his elbow on the rough table pitches forward toward the shot, as if falling into water. Blood squirts in a two-foot-high arc from the back of his head; bright, metallic-looking in the lamplight. I back away, pushing the man's twitching body from me, bloodying my hands and the pistol in the process.

From farther back in the room flat-faced women and big-eyed children gape at me. One young woman breathes in loud open-mouthed gasps. The strange marine has disappeared now, like a shadow, gone and no trace of him. I drop my lantern in the dust of the floor, back into the darkness until I reach a wall, turn and search for the opening, fall into the light of day, gasping for breath.

Nim sounds far away, yet he's right here grasping my shoulders. "Are you having an attack, Don? Are you asthmatic?"

I suck in one last shuddery breath, look up, smile. "I'm fine. Just had one. You know. One of those things, right here. It's been a long time since that one."

"My goodness. I think you may be suffering more than usual stress in your life, Don."

"I get over these things quickly, usually quickly." We are both on our feet. I clasp his hand, look up into his eyes.

"Thank you!" I leave now, without another word.

❧
Chapter Ten

My wife is lying there in her—not our—king-size bed, that bed in which I have longed to lie with her, holding her, comforting her. She is partially under the quilt—the blue one with the appliqué embroidery my ex-student and Mitzi's little weeping cousin Bootsie Dwindle bestowed on me in remembrance of my retirement. The quilt appears to have been thrown over Mitzi up to the waist. Must have taken Bootsie hours to do all that sewing. I now recognize the quilt as symbolic.

Mitzi's hands are arranged, not clasped, one over the other on her breast. You can see the green fingernails, fresh polish probably. Green to match The Giant. Her eyes are closed. She looks beautiful in the fluffy-ruffled yellow nightgown I bought at Runcibles in the Mall in Delta City for her birthday just a year ago. Yellow ribbon interlaced around the bodice. ("Ruffles on sleepwear are uncomfortable," she complained at the time of receiving.) Hair mussed, but face unwrinkled and innocent-looking, the way she's always wanted her face to look on the TV.

She is dead. She has died and the husband for some reason was not present to witness the departure—not present except in spirit.

And here's usually cheerful Kork, too, almost running in place here in her bedroom—he in his jogging shorts and his hairy bare chest, telling Constable Cod, "We was having a cuppa coffee is all," he is saying, "and she craps out. Just like that." There are no cups of coffee to be seen in the bedroom. Perhaps they had the coffee before their seamy romp. Or perhaps it was to be afterwards, a post-coital celebratory coffee. It must have been her heart. A weak heart, even after all that jogging. Why Kork? She's never been interested in Coach Kork Sporlodden. She's always derided his consultant cards showered repeatedly on friends and acquaintances—and on strangers in the street.

Is this one real? I avert my eyes from the acidic gaze of Ab Crinkle glowering at me, instead observe the numbers in the radio across the room, easily visible to one of superior eyesight, even with their fuzzy red color. They at once sound a *flick*, metamorphose into 7:00, and stimulate mellow tones from KDC-FM.

Lamont groans, stretches, smacks his lips, opens his eyes at me, rolls his body off my feet. Mitzi has probably long since risen for her jog. One would never wonder what Chum finds interesting about Mitzi; one might wonder what Mitzi finds interesting about Chum, especially with Chum already having a dear friend in Audrey Frackle.

Again, is this one finally real? No, it's not real. I can feel the stubble on my jaw; amazing that I should grow whiskers so rapidly. I can feel the grit under my eyelids. The scene and cast? Another one of those fantasies, or dreams, or "thoughts" that persons of a certain history are doomed to have, if one believes the literature as an educated person is wont to do. But what meaning does the scene present? Of course it's obvious what it *means,* fool. It means you are again manifesting those self-doubts about which you will warn your counselees.

I shorten my time in the shower to avoid a confrontation with Mitzi. She and Chum will want to shower together as fellow athletes. They will desire plenty of hot water. I put on blue sweats and white athletic sox, not that I plan to run this morning. I do that only three times weekly. The sweats are because Mitzi insists on keeping the house cool, compensating for Mother Crinkle's exorbitant use of her bedroom's personal electric appliances. Thanksgiving in only one week. I start the hot water kettle, relishing briefly the warmth of the gas flame on my hands. Winter promises to be chill.

The tears come unbidden at the kitchen table, overflowing onto cheeks and chin and page while I'm drinking my breakfast tea and reading Mr. D.H. Carp's latest column in last Tuesday's *Courier*, tears precipitated by I don't know what. Probably not by Mr. Carp who is going on about how well he will serve us if we send him to Congress.

Suddenly before me across the quiet room, frilly-yellow-curtain-filtered sunrise just beginning to creep onto my table, presaging an actually sunny day, there is would-be third-baseman Tedley, trying to stanch the spurting stump with his floppy, his mocha-brown face frowning at where the rest of his arm used to be. No screaming. He struts from the treeline back into the jungle shouting for our corpsman. "Feathers! I guess I got a job for you, Feathers!"

And the new lieutenant whose name we didn't quite catch, gold bar still shiny in its little box back at base, standing there briefly and then collapsing to his knees where he had been staring at his executioner winking down at us from 500 meters into the sun. The headless neck unbelievably frothing, whistling, the arms flailing and legs kicking and quivering in the red mud. Like something from a movie gunfight, only much, much moreso. Futures, dreams, lives all over with in ten seconds. "Friendly fire" they would call it. Where am I? Where am I?

Jungle trail again. Different trail; different time. Nim five meters behind, carrying extra ammo because he volunteered to be the mule. Feathers humming, Breene complaining about the heat and the insects, Vitale complaining about Feathers' humming, I thinking about what it would be like to have a bath in a long bathtub with fragrant bathsalts. Breene's irritable trumpet voice from behind us ordering Ace forward.

Ace comes forward, he comes forward, he comes forward. The face is Asian, collapsed, not a marine after all. Ace wags his head. No way he's going to "probe the body." This is a classic field-manual booby-trap situation. He kneels, lowers his pack, searches for twine or wire or rope to attach to the corpse's arm or leg, prepares to test his hypothesis.

Breene hurries up. "For Chrissakes, Bernsteen! You goddam slowpoke." Horrified, we watch Breene's foot come back and then snap forward in a kick. "No!" shouts Nim, too late. The explosion is much louder than one would expect. Perhaps they wanted to provide a special lesson for us. Ace is shredded, as is Breene. I am blinded with the sheen from those two closest, now mostly disappeared except for rags visible on bushes and trees and in the long grass. I wipe my eyes. The hand before my face is covered with blood, palm and back. Nim is down. With greater distance from the blast I have been spared.

I am standing, feel no pain. Feel nothing at all. My ears ring. My entire front is wet. First time that's happened. Probably I have urinated at the blast, as well as absorbed a lot of flying blood. I unbuckle and drop my pack; for no reason at all I walk in a circle. Feathers shouts at me, "Lay down, Keyhole! Lay down. You're hit." I can see that Feathers is hit himself, bleeding from the scalp and face. He works on Nim, bleeding on his patient. Tourniquet applied. Nim's eyes are closed; he is frowning, a rare expression for Nim. Is he dead? Vitale is screaming into the radio for lift-out.

Feathers works on me. "Jesus, Keyhole. Can you still hold this compress? Good! Hold it down hard as you can! I never seen this before. Jesus!" Feathers has lost his professional cool. "No, don't try to look. You been hit...so just hold this tight. Jesus!" He's bleeding on me now as he plunges the styrette into my leg, the first followed by a second.

I don't find out what-all I've lost until I wake up at base.

Suddenly back again, cup in hand, sunlight glowing on the white saucer, I rise to bring in this morning's *Courier*, almost resolved to write my own column. About what? What at long last can I write about that people can read with their breakfast?

✲ Chapter Eleven

The sounds and smells are strangely far away but becoming gradually closer, more discernible, as when arriving on foot at a familiar neighborhood. My back hurts, my head hurts, my shoulder hurts, my neck hurts. Am I dreaming again of wounds, dreaming of the jungle? I fumble at my shirt for an aspirin, feel unfamiliar garments commingled with the pain that accompanies the movement. I had stooped to pick up this morning's *Courier;* I awaken to the startlingly blue eyes of Nimitz Chaud. He's leaning forward in an armless metal chair, hands on his knees. Behind him is a shiny green wall. I'm in a hospital. I'm dreaming again.

I can hear myself breathing. "I'm dreaming again."

"You're not dreaming, Don. You're in Doctors Hospital in Delta City. Do you remember anything about what happened or about getting here?"

"Wha?" All I can manage with my dry mouth is that one part-word. My eyes hurt. My mouth hurts. I manage to get the sound out. "What?" Mitzi has shot me for being a wimp. It was she with the paste or rubber cement. She's disposed of me at last but I am clinging to life, attended by my only friend. I didn't even know she had a pistol. How foolish not to have searched diligently for a weapon after her outbursts.

No, it's not a gunshot wound. I have had a heart attack. That's why my neck and shoulder ache. I should have taken more aspirin. It's what all the literature says: take aspirin! But I have ignored the literature to my detriment.

Or probably I have had a stroke and am dying. I can feel life slipping away, like water running down my arm in the shower, dripping off my fingers, getting the toilet seat wet again. Mitzi will complain about that. My family are clustered around the bed, waiting to hear the will read by a notary.

I don't have a family, except for Mitzi. I've never completed the process of writing my will. I don't know a notary. That scene is something out of *Gianni Schicchi*. I groan; at least the sound is authentic. What's wrong with me? Why am I here? I should ask. I don't have to ask.

"You were attacked, Don. You were hit on the head, several good licks of a blunt object, probably by a very strong person, the doctors say. Mitzi found you head-down in your front-porch azaleas and called the ambulance—and then called me, for which I'm grateful. I called Quince Runcible to look in on you when they finished wrapping you up."

"I was attacked? Who was it? Jess Pleroma?"

"Was it Jess?"

"I'm asking, was it?"

"Nobody seems to know, Don. This would be the first time that Jess has ever attacked anybody physically. Why do you mention Jess?"

"Seemed like a good idea." My head hurts when I try to move it, when I try to think. "Maybe it was Junior Trilbend?"

"I think probably you're not supposed to move your head just now. It's all bandaged up. No, just leave it alone. They want you to stay very still for a while, until they figure out how serious your injuries are. They're looking at the x-rays again. Junior Trilbend? Junior would come at you straight on, but only if you were smaller and weaker. I doubt that Junior would attack a six-foot-two ex-marine who is still in good shape—even wimpish!"

He grins. He frowns. "But then, we never know everything about people, do we."

I peek down under the sheet. "I hope not." I'm wearing a hospital gown. My spirits sink. "They undressed me. The nurses undressed me."

"Sure. They removed your shoes, too. You're in hospital, Don. We always get undressed in hospitals, you and I. Remember?"

He knows better than to tell me not to worry about it. He's making light of my situation.

"I wonder, is Lamont all right? Was Lamont attacked?"

"I don't know, Don, but I'll find out. If he's okay I'll take him home with me during your stay here, if it's all right with Mitzi."

"Is Mitzi all right? Mitzi isn't here? Did Mitzi get hurt, too?" I don't ask if it was Mitzi who attacked me. That would be too shameful. I am ashamed, for I asked first about Lamont.

"This is Saturday, Don. Mitzi's doing her sportscar rally today. She did the paperwork so they'd let you in here without the sack of gold in advance. She said she figures you're going to be fine, so why should she hang around with nothing to do but look sad and worried? A strong woman with a good argument, don't you think?"

I don't think so, but I don't feel like saying so. Instead, I say, "I guess the wimp-note has come true."

"Well, you're not dead, Don. So the note has not come true after all. Maybe the note has nothing to do with this. Let's take some time to figure things out; not jump to any conclusions. Constable Cod is looking into things. He may call in the sheriff."

"You can't go in there!" is the cry from the hallway where I can get a glimpse of a nurse trying to halt the progress of a tall blond young man in a leather jacket. It's Joseph Kuhl peering in the doorway.

"I'm Mr. Keyshot's official private investigator with some stuff to maybe report." Joe explains this to several people who are hurrying by. The nurse has been signalled by Pastor Nim and has departed, leaving Joseph standing as he entered, now leaning against the door frame. "Dang! I need a badge. Jeez, you look terrible, Mr. Keyshot. What a huge bandage there. You look like an Arab just washed his hair with your towel like that. Is he gonna die?" This last to Nim, I suppose.

"Eventually, I expect, like the rest of us. But for now, he's expected to live well and prosper." Nim makes the split-hand Spock gesture. I have never been able to get my hand into that position. Nim is flexible and optimistic.

"Hey, yeh." Joseph sits himself on the foot of the bed, jarring me and causing a spontaneous groan. "I ran over one of those dumb bumps in the parking lot down there. Hit too fast. Probably caused my alignment to unalign." He demonstrates the misalignment with his body, thus eliciting another groan from me.

"Perhaps you could take it easy on the movement there, Joe," says Nim.

"Uh, yeh. Sorry. You know who the perp was did it?"

"It's a mystery perp at this point, we guess."

Nim shrugs his shoulders.

Joe is biting on sunflower seeds, spitting the hulls into his hand, chewing the product in the front of his mouth. My dry mouth suddenly waters. If I have any addiction, it's to sunflower seeds.

"Probably Jess Pleroma. Probably start there."

"Why there, Joe?"

"Well, Jess's known for crimes and misdemeanors around Balona, so what I mean is, when there's one to solve, you think of the first natural one to suspect." He lowers his voice and leans confidentially on my catheter tube. "That's a criminal justice procedure you learn in criminal justice."

"Ah." This from both Nim and me.

"I'm assigning myself to this crime, pro-bono."

"That's very kind of you, Joseph."

"Well, you probably don't got a lot of money, so...."

"You'll maybe be working with Constable Cod and the sheriff's deputies, though."

"Huh? Oh, yeh. Them. Yeh, they're, uh, sort of old friends of mine. What I mean is, professional associates, y'know. Warren and Paul. They're both sergeants now, y'know, but they still work together, like a team. My Uncle Anson says he won't break 'em up." Sheriff Anson Chaud is Joseph's uncle on his mother's side. Joseph has relatives in all sorts of high places in Chaud County, a fact which has not necessarily benefited Joe's ethical and moral development.

"That sounds good to me." Nim has known those young officers since they were children. I know them by sight.

"So, but I need to get some facts on this perpetrator, Mr. Keyshot. So, again, what I mean is, what did he look like?" Joe raises one eyebrow, squints his eyes, appearing suddenly very detectivish.

"I believe I already mentioned, Joseph, I didn't get a look. Didn't even know I'd been attacked until I woke up in this bed."

"All right! He must've whacked you good. Probably a blunt-force instrument. What I mean is, whatever it was he hit you with was blunt."

"And forceful." This from Nim, smiling.

"And forceful, sure. That's why we always say *blunt force*. Of course." He extracts a spiral notebook from his jacket, scribbles in it for a moment, mouthing the words: "...blunt force of course." He looks up, explains. "It rhymes, so I write it down and then look in it later when I'm pondering and writing poems. Like a bank, sort of. It's what Shakespeare and those guys did, most of 'em."

"Well, then, you're in good company, Joseph."

"Yeh. Well, I better get back to Balona and do some investigating. Is it okay I go over to your house and interrogate your wife?"

"I believe she's out on the road today, Joseph, doing a rally."

"Oh, yeh. Sammy Jack Sly's doing it in his Jag. Dang, I forgot! I was supposed to ride with him and do something with maps, but when I heard about Mr. Keyshot getting shot or stabbed or clobbered by a mysterious perpetrator over there, I rushed on over to see what I could find out. Uh, is there a reward pending, you think? What I mean is, they usually say *reward pending* when there's maybe a reward. Pending."

Nim responds to this. "The virtue you are demonstrating is its own reward, Joseph. Remember?" They are apparently referring to some lesson Nim gives at Tabernacle.

"Oh, yeh. Well, pending means hanging or hung up, so I guess it's hung up." Joe seems keenly disappointed at the prospect of a hung-up reward. He rises from my bed carefully, rearranges the catheter tube more neatly, but pulls on it so that it now spills bodily fluid onto the floor instead of into its plastic receptacle. Nim replaces the tube and presses the button for the nurse. "Well, I guess I've did enough virtue for today anyways, so tootle-oo—that's a new saying we got at C4? Tootle-oo? It's actually a foreign language saying, means *see you around*. So, I'll stay in touch." Joe disappears.

"Is there anything you'd like me to take care of, Don, besides looking after Lamont? I have plenty of time this afternoon. My sermon for tomorrow is all outlined and I was planning to sit around reading poetry and listening to music tonight."

"I'd just like to know that Mitzi is okay and that whoever did this to me isn't out for her, too."

"That surely has occurred to law enforcement, and I'll bet they're going to keep an eye on her. She should be home from her rally by now. I imagine Quince Runcible will be looking in on you soon. I saw him down in the lobby."

"Right here! How's things, men?" Doctor Quince Runcible is not as big as Nim and not bearded or mustached, but he gives the same golden impression. He is one of those people that even the meanest of Balona mothers wish their children had become or would marry or would be friends with.

"How's things, Quince?"

"You feeling a little better, Don?"

"Not feeling much at all, except for a toothache and a headache and a shoulder ache. And a backache."

"All consistent with your recent trauma, I'd say. Doctor Bronk did the workup on you, says it doesn't look serious, says you have a very hard head." The doctor crinkles his eyes at us, shows his teeth. Not at all a constipated smile. "I would suspect you'll spend maybe tonight here and be released in the morning, if there are no complications." He frowns. "You remember yet who smacked you?"

I start to shake my head, make a negative face instead.

"Well, it may come back to you. The identity of the attacker, I mean. Injuries like this sometimes produce immediate amnesia and subsequent recollection. But then I needn't tell either of you fellows about that. The trickle working all right?"

The catheter was probably Quince's suggestion and I thank him for his thoughtfulness. The two of them leave, laughing in the hall.

Chapter Twelve

When you are in hospital you spend most of your time thinking. You may try not to, but there's nothing much else to do, so there you are. If you are in pain, you think about when it's going to stop. If you're not in pain, you think about other things previously on your mind. I got around to thinking about Mitzi and our relationship, and Mitzi's relationships and job searches and amusements, and why she hasn't yet been to see me.

We do have an odd relationship, but it's understandable when you know the facts and don't merely speculate, the way most residents of Balona are wont to speculate about other people's marriages, children, fashions in haircuts, drinking habits, sexual preference, and choice of dog.

It was Mitzi who courted me. Courted is an old-fashioned word, I know, but that's what it amounted to. I had written her a note, complimenting her news-anchoring, telling her she was my favorite anchorperson of all time. That was true. She is tall, blonde, and very pretty. Lively. Sparkly-eyed. I think the best word is *vivacious,* which means (as Joe Kuhl would say) full of life.

In my note I told her I was a high school counselor of a "certain age" who lived alone, watched only the news on TV, and was otherwise entertained by good books. It was not a pitch for sex or a date or even for a response. I'm sure women who perform on TV receive many notes from men, including offers of marriage, invitations to parties of all kinds, and compliments.

Probably few complaints. I didn't expect a response, as I routinely write notes to authors, politicians, musicians, students, the parents of students—to people I admire or whose work has somehow touched me favorably.

I was surprised to get a phone call from her at my office. "It's Mitzi Crinkle on the phone for you, Mr. Keyshot! Line one." Candy Wishingfor's big blue eyes were open wide as she shouted the news across the office.

"Is this Mr. Keyshot of Balona High School fame?" Mitzi's voice is low and sweet; I recognized it at once.

"It is indeed, Miss Crinkle. How may I help you?" This is what I always said to callers, some of them irritated with something the school had done (or not done) or their child had done (or not done).

"Well, how's things?" This was a surprise—her greeting me in the Balona idiom.

"Well, how's things?" This is the proper Balona reponse.

"Well, dit'n you know I'm an alumni of Big Baloney and that I live over there with you guys?"

"My goodness! I didn't know that." She does have Balonan speech peculiarities, tolerated nowdays by TV where one hears all sorts of accents and problems of articulation, but it was true that I did not know Mitzi's alumna status. No one to my knowledge had ever claimed Mitzi Crinkle to be a product of Balona High and a resident. A surprise. An organization—especially a school that is preparing young people for the world of work—should celebrate its successful products.

"I appreciated your note."

"Well, it's heartfelt, and I just wanted you to know you have this additional fan—among many, I'm sure." I didn't know what else to say. What do you say to a famous person but that you appreciate what he or she is famous for?

"I would like to buy you a cup of coffee."

"My goodness! Well, sure. I'm always thirsty." I made a little joke there as I was feeling quite warm and fuzzy.

"How's about this afternoon at Frank's at, say, five?"

I never got off until after five usually, but I figured I could sneak myself away once, as nobody ever paid attention to when I came in and went home—as it was always earlier and later than anybody else. "Sure."

"Well, okay, then." Silence. "So I'll see you there and then."

"Well, okay, then."

She didn't ask what I looked like or whether I'd be wearing a lily in my lapel. Simple as that, she must have assumed I would recognize and approach her, as it was obvious from my note that I was familiar with her appearance.

At five I was sitting in one of Frank's booths watching the door. Frank's *Soupe de Jour* is bad French and greasy hamburgers, but very well-boiled coffee. Frank Backhouse, too, is a product of Balona High, he (according to Frank himself) having been known as the Hound of the Basketballs during his student days.

Frank has been, and continues to be, celebrated as a Balona alumnus. Perhaps athletes are more memorable than musicians or artists or chemists or lawyers.

Frank served me a cuppa, reminded me that I had told him some time ago that I, too, had played and lettered at basketball in high school but undoubtedly not as well as Frank is reputed to have done at the sport.

Frank asked what else I wanted to accompany the coffee.

"I'll be joined by a young woman soon, I hope."

"Oh, yeh? Well, good luck and, y'know, don't get too, y'know, involved. They'll suck you dry those, y'know, young women. And when they get old, y'know, they never remember the old days when you thrilled 'em with, y'know, great shots on the court." Frank evidently doesn't *feel* his celebrity keenly nowdays. "They always want to know what they're gonna, y'know, get next. And that has always got to be, y'know, *something new*. So, just keep that in mind when you're being, y'know, joined here by that young woman."

Frank has a melancholy look to accompany his athlete's habits of speech; he's possibly another potential client. Gossip which I try not to listen to has Frank and his wife frequently at odds, the wife accusing him publicly of trying to poison her with the leftovers he takes home from the Soupe de Jour. Frank's mournful look brightens as he sees my aforesaid young woman guest enter through the jingling door. The old fellows drinking coffee and talking baseball in loud voices at the counter fall silent, hold their coffee cups midair, watch the arrival.

I rise, step forward. "Don Keyshot, Miss Crinkle."

"Ah." She holds her hand out, palm down as if to be kissed. I almost do, but press it instead. "I've started already I'm afraid."

"Well, Frank's coffee is so famous, I shut'n wonder. How's things, Frank?"

"How's things, Mitzi?" Frank blushes from his great height. Mitzi sits, pulls off her mittens. (At the time it was January and the delta fog is heavy, ground-hugging, and especially chill that time of the year.)

"You're the famous Mr. Keyshot." She examines me, my yellow wrinkled face, my whitening hair, my gaunt looks. I do have good teeth, splendid vision, and unequalled hearing. "I've seen you around, you know. You have a lot of character in your face."

"I've been told I'm a character. You have great beauty in yours."

"Some of the suits say so, too; some don't think so. Some think I'm getting old."

"Well, we're all getting older, but some of us don't seem to show it." I crinkle my eyes. Crinkle at Miss Crinkle. "Not I, of course."

"Quince says you're a very nice guy, a tolerant, flexible guy."

"Quince. Doctor Runcible?" I hope Doctor Runcible hasn't been telling tales out of the office.

"I went to school with Quince—yes, at Big Baloney! We've stayed in touch. He said I ought to look you up."

"Why in the world would he say that? I'm the last guy you could imagine being a media-type guy. I don't even watch TV, except for *Mitzi Crinkle and the News and Mitzi Crinkle's Garden* and *Mitzi Crinkle's Bookshelf.*"

"Well, how nice. Quince dit'n exactly say I should look you up. That was a literature license I used just then. What he said was, you have some characteristics I could get used to. Characteristics lots of other men don't have, like, for example patience and tolerance and you don't need to grope and hug and kiss all the time—and that I should consider getting to know you."

She takes a sip of coffee, wrinkles her nose, pushes the cup away. "Used to Starbuck's, I guess," she explains. She lowers her voice. "My mother tells me I need to get married or she'll throw me out of the house, so I been trying to find the right man. You're about the only Balona guy isn't blood-related to me one way or another."

This out of the blue. This is obviously a New Woman, but I try to retain my self-assured expression. "My mother told me I should get married, too, a long time ago. I ignored her, and look at me now."

"Yes, I'm looking. You've surely got the pick of anybody you might want."

"Quince says of all the people he knows, you're the one might like to be married the most, but he's of the opinion you will probably never ask a woman to be your wife."

"Perhaps you're aware how unusual this conversation is."

"Your face is turning pink. Very attractive." She's reversing our roles here, very much as I would have predicted if this were a conversation for the stage, not a real life situation with two people who have never before spoken to each other.

"Well, I know you find me gorgeous. You as much as told me so in your note. I don't get many notes as revealing as that one. Almost expected roses to come with it. But that's not your style, is it? You don't *go after* a woman, do you? You just compliment them to make them feel good."

"I write notes to people who do especially good work, who make me feel good about their competence and the state of the world. Actually, I send quite a few to students and parents."

"I know about that, too. I have spies all over Balona." She leans back and looks me over, including my fingernails. You are very clean."

"I learned good habits a long time ago." I am falling in love with this woman. Maybe it's the shots working overtime. Maybe I should reduce the shots. Maybe I should tell her I would very much like to grope and hug and kiss. I need to consult with Quince.

"You learned good habits from your mother?"

"From my Uncle Sam."

"Ah, yes. Quince mentioned that you were a marine. You don't look like a marine."

"What does a marine look like?"

"Wears a blue coat and a white hat."

"I have some gear like that in my closet at home."

"In the closet? Your history is in the closet?"

"In the closet."

"Me, too."

"I beg your pardon. Good heavens, were you a marine? You don't look like a marine!"

"Touché. But no, not that. I'll tell you some time."

"We're having another date?"

"Oh, I hope so. I find you to be just about what I want the man in my life to be. Do you think we could get along?"

I felt like a teenager must feel when so touched.

We met again, of course, and she told me her secret, and I told her mine, and she said she already figured it out, and we agreed to marry and share a life. "My mother will live with us, of course, in my house. She'll have her own room, just like you'll have your own room."

"Uh, I see. Well, of course, if that's the way you want it."

"She is very old, but a strong woman still, and very opinionated. You may not like her. She's pretty critical.

"I'm a public school employee. I'm used to criticism."

And it was settled. Nim was surprised and at first puzzled, then happy for me. Mitzi came to several faculty parties and was appropriately admired. It happened that we were married on the very day Mitzi lost her job. The faculty believed the firing but were unbelieving about the marriage until the item appeared in both the Delta City *Beacon* and the Balona *Courier*.

Mr. Sam John Sly is not only Chairman of the Board of the King Korndog Korporation, he is a part-owner of KDC-TV, the station whose owners dismissed Mitzi.

Perhaps he felt guilty. He made us a week-long, all-expenses-paid gift of his boat.

And we did not grope and hug and kiss after all. Chum accompanied us on our nuptial boat trip down the Yulumne, selecting the food, preparing some of it, joining us at table, drinking many a toast, piloting the boat, and sleeping with the bride.

Chapter Thirteen

A hearty red-haired nurse handed me the cane as I arose from the obligatory wheelchair in the lobby of Doctors Hospital. "I don't need a cane either, for heavensakes," I said, laughing and pushing the thing aside. It will be on my bill, I'm sure.

But the nurse said, "Hospital rules, and we don't want to be difficult, do we?" I pride myself on never being difficult. I wasn't even difficult when I was in hospital 30 years ago and had more reason to be difficult.

Nim came for me on the bus, and on the bus we made our return to Balona. He no longer owns a vehicle and, when not riding his bicycle or walking, almost always uses public transportation, such as it is. And I, well, neither do I own a vehicle.

Where was Mitzi?

Nim and I gimped our way from the bus stop, and he left me at the foot of my office stairs. (Balona residents no longer enjoy the convenience of an actual station, a result of corporate down-sizing which is often known to up-size the wallets of the stockholders.) "Your cane seems a little short for you, Don," he had observed on the way over. "Let me adjust it." Whereupon he loosened then tightened some rings on the cane and did something to some buttons on the metal shaft and lo! I was able to rest on it standing straight up. The cane was helpful. Also felt much better, not leaning 40 degrees to the windward. "I hope we'll be seeing more of you at Tabernacle, Don."

It is not possible to deny Nimitz Chaud.

I tottered into Tabernacle for Wednesday evening service, head still arabesque but limping straightly, having walked all the way from Front Street, where Lamont and I have established permanent residence in my office. My head still aches, and my neck and shoulder. The back and leg, too, probably from he many scratches when I fell into the shrubbery after the attack.

Except for Front Street where mercury vapor casts its ghastly glow, only the occasional residence porch light illuminates the rest of Balona's foggy November streets. Should I have walked unaccompanied all the way from Front Street to First Avenue and then down First to Tabernacle? A long walk in the dark for one who is recovering from assault by a still-anonymous villain who attacks from the rear. I have come to enjoy tempting fate, perhaps to see if anything else will happen to me. I have thought about sending away for one of those canes that conceal a sword. I could write a novel. A romance: The Swordsman of Balona. Some swordsman.

For the evening service only a dozen-or-so people were in attendance. I didn't see Bellona Shaw's red coiffure. Birdie Swainhammer at the organ was noodling "My Funny Valentine," and the congregation turned as I entered. They stood up and applauded! This was surely arranged.

"Welcome, Don. Welcome to Tabernacle, in the brotherhood of man, under the fatherhood of God." Nim really believes in this stuff, which is why he has maintained the name "BoMFoG" for his organization, despite some growing opposition from younger members of his congregation who come right out and say "it sounds dumb."

Then followed a few minutes during which he kept me standing in the aisle in front of the lectern while he went on about how I was a good fellow and a buddy from way back and had done good things to help a lot of needful Balonans, young and old. The people applauded several times and I blushed a lot and shuffled my feet.

"You can be seated, Don, now that we've welcomed you back into the land of the living." And everybody laughed. Ms Penny Preene and her daughter Claire pulled me down to sit beside them in the front pew and we all listened to Nim read selections from the Anglican Book of Common Prayer, not your typical Tabernacle fare, but beautiful. Unusual, as usual. That's Nim's style. Then there was a hymn, and Birdie segued into a *vox humana* version of "People Who Need People" as her closing.

Afterward, all of them shook my hand. All of them looked me in the eye and shook my hand. Did I feel like weeping in relief and gratitude that at least these folks didn't see me as some kind of pervert? Yes, but I "kept my suave," as Balona youth are wont to say.

Mrs. Applehanger touched my sleeve to stop my progress out of Tabernacle, reached in her handbag, and presented me with one of her famous foil-wrapped fruitcakes. The generic fruitcake for some reason has become an object of ridicule in some circles, possibly because of the often miserable examples of the product sold by mail. But an Applehanger fruitcake is home-made, fresh and moist, and full of all manner of wholesome fruits and nuts. Besides, Mrs. Applehanger tends to extend the life of her products by dosing them liberally with rum, not to speak of another herb cosseted in Aunty Pring Chaud's greenhouse that causes much mirth without evident reason, a generally relaxed feeling, and a stimulated appetite. I pressed her arm and squinted my eyes at her while stuffing her gift into my raincoat pocket.

"We intend to take care of you, Mr. Keyshot. Bellona Shaw says she's going to help, too, even though she's not yet a member of the congregation." At this, Mrs. Applehanger winked a great wink at me and clucked. "We figure you're probably due to be alone for a while, you know." Word does get around.

After the service I caned my way back to my apartment, lighter in spirit. Lamont greeted me at the top of the stairs and indicated that now *he* wished to make a trek. We toured Front Street and Balona Park where Lamont deposited major spoor, and Good Citizen Don transferred it via our new Scooper to a trash can.

Out of the corner of my eye I caught a flash of a dark-clothed individual, seemingly keeping to the shadows, undoubtedly following us. I felt at once the need to hit the deck, lock and load, a learned behavior hard to excise. But I decided against retreat. Instead, I advanced upon the shrubbery that was concealing my follower, cane at the ready in one hand, Scooper in the other, Lamont beside me, Lamont now wagging his tail, disappointing behavior in an attack dog on the job.

I stopped and elocuted in my hardest voice, "You might as well come out of there. I see you. Show your face." It occurred to me that I might tack on the coda, "or I'm coming in there to drag you out," but good sense prevailed.

"Oh." The tone rang as disappointed. "You seen, uh, saw me after all. I was tailing you, keeping an eye out, y'know." It was Joseph Kuhl in dark jeans, dark jacket, dark shoes, a knit cap pulled down over his face, the type with the embroidered eye-holes and "O" mouth popularized by television terrorists.

Lamont was sniffing in a friendly way. "You gave me a start, Joseph. I thought for a moment you were the person who attacked me. I was about ready to counter-whack you a good one with my cane here."

"Oh, geez! I'm sorry. I was protecting you. You know, pro-bono like. The way I said? Well, I guess you're okay, so my duty is done and I'll just melt away into the dark."

"Uh, Joe? May I make a suggestion? Perhaps you could remove the cap, or at least fold it up. Don't you think it might terrify a much older or much younger person seeing it on a tall man emerging from the bushes in the dark?"

"Hey, yeh! I never thought of that." In fact he sounded delighted at the prospect of terrifying an older or younger person. "Well, tootle-oo." He melted into the bushes, disappeared.

Where was Mitzi?

Mitzi was in San Francisco, by ordinary driver two hours away on the Interstates across the Altamont, the Oakland Hills, and the Bay Bridge—only seventy minutes with Mitzi at the wheel of the Green Giant.

Mitzi left her note unsealed at the hospital rece   p-tion desk with instructions to "deliver to Don Keyshot when he wakes up." The text revealed that she was sure I would recover nicely, what with the well-known hardness of my head, and that Chum and she were appointed to a particular celebration involving women, leather, champagne, and television. Mitzi would stay.

> *Chum's going back to work, of course, but I'll probably be moving to SF for good if this interview turns out, so you can do what you want with Daddy's furniture and what's in the fridge, ect. Iris is supposed to break the news to Mama and get somebody to move in with her to take care of her, since it's legally her house. Chum isn't inter-ested in that job. Sorry about this, but it's the way I am. You know. Sorry.*

"Iris" is Mitzi's very much older half-sister (and Boot-sie's grandmother). The remarkable reference to

"Daddy's furniture" is probably the heavy mahogany bedstead in "Daddy's bedroom." I couldn't possibly want it for my own. I couldn't even lift it. But the furniture offer and the twice-employed "sorry" is Mitzi's way of demonstrating that she is a person of conscience who doesn't only take, but also gives.

The way the nurses looked at me and buzzed behind their hands indicated that her note had been passed around enough so that my situation was well known.

Quince Runcible had come by just before I left the hospital. He had pulled on his lip and mumbled, "Sorry for your trouble, Don. I thought she was more stable nowadays," further strengthening my belief that Mitzi has somethng of a history.

I fluffed-up Lamont's box-pillows, made myself a cup of tea, and sat down to preview my appointments for the week, such as they are: Junior Trilbend and his sidekick Bobby R. Langsam, whom the county insists I see as a "group," possibly to save them some money. I must educate county authorities. A man and wife from family court in Delta City who evidently don't want to be seen by their neighbors going to a Delta City practitioner. A child and her mother from Balona High School, which is a nice touch after all the miserable rumors. And Mrs. Shaw again, probably only to complete her interview, but perhaps to pursue her dream.

I chewed on an aspirin and considered the half of the glass that's full.

Chapter Fourteen

"There's no need for excuses, Mrs. Shaw. I am here at your pleasure, whatever it may be." I say this while ushering the lady into my office, now crowded somewhat with my cot and Lamont's trappings, a footlocker, a chest of drawers, and an oversize cardboard armoire for my clothes. All of it still requires some squaring away. Perhaps *pleasure* was the wrong word for me to use just now, as I noticed Mrs. Shaw's eyes become beady as the word came out.

"Well, I certainly appreciate you making the time, especially on such short notice, eksedra." Mrs. Shaw made this appointment last week. Mrs. Shaw is obviously flustered. She turns completely about, looks around the room. "I've been having these dreams, you see. So this isn't exactly a journalism call, you see."

"Mm-hm." I have seated her in my client's chair so that we are almost knee to knee, except for the low table between us that holds the requisite holder with its box of tissues, the holder a gift of Pastor Nim in honor of my new practice. She eyes the tissues.

"I guess you have people here that use quite a few of those."

"It's been a useful invention, the tissue." I squint my eyes humorously, sympathetically. I settle back in my chair, prepare again to feast on someone else's troubles. "The dreams, you said," I prompt.

She blushes. "Did I say dreams? Oh, well, yas. Well, they're—how shall I say it—uh, like the dreams a young person usually has, although you could hardly consider me a young person." She peers at me over her half-glasses but I ignore the gambit out of professional discretion. "You know."

"You could describe one of those dreams."

"I was actually thinking about finishing our first interview so I could write you up. For the *Courier*, y'know."

"Well, either way, I'm right here for you."

"You're bigger than I thought. I mean, you never did *strike* me like a big man, but then, when I look at you—certainly when I stand next to you—I have to look way up at you and you look, you look, uh, really much bigger."

"That's probably because I'm tall even though skinny. And I try never to *strike* women!"

"That's what I meant. Big, like." She ignores my humor.

"About the dreams...."

"I got into the journalism business sort of by accident."

"It was accidental." My technique here is what is known as *non-directive,* a distinctly old-fashioned style that comports with my view of what therapeutic counseling should be about.

Nim Chaud still uses the same technique very effectively. Didn't work on Mr. D.H. Carp, but might with somebody else unsuspecting.

"I was looking for a job and I walked into the *Courier* office, and Mr. Patrick Preene just happened to be looking for somebody to do gardens and pets and society. That sort of thing. Just an accident."

"And that's it. Fortuitous."

"No, accidental; and I was feeling sort of low."

"Mm-hm. Low."

"Actually, Mr. Preene's brother sent me to the newspaper."

"Old Pastor Preene."

"That's the one. Except not so very old." Mrs. Shaw looks at the table, frowns. "He was a really fine man, whatever people say nowdays."

"People say?"

"They say he was a sex fiend. Not a nice thing to say about a pastor, and dead at that."

"Not nice at all."

"Of course he was a sex fiend, but in a nice way, y'know?"

"A nice sex fiend."

"He put your troubles to rest in a nice way. Your fingers are quite long. Maybe you play the piano?" She's changing the subject.

"About the dreams."

"About the dreams? Well, they're, uh, erotic, you might say."

"Yes. Erotic dreams." Now I proceed to temporize, break the train of thought with my tedious (as Mitzi describes it) tendency to overwhelm people with explanations: "Many people have such dreams regularly, a regular part of their nights." I nod my head sagely. I recall reading somewhere that a counselor's best technique is the listening technique, not the explaining technique. I need to improve my technique.

"You can't see out of your window from here." Her tone is complaining, not simple observing.

"Well, not while you're sitting you can't. But one is able to stand at the window there and see all of Front Street, provided you hang your head out of the window." I'm explaining again. I need to control that.

"You have a very nice mouth, you know."

"How's that?" This is a surprise. First the "handsome man" bit; now this.

"My erotic dream was about...about...about me and Jess Pleroma, young Jess Pleroma, the young fellow I told you about who I hoped was harassing me?"

"Pardon? You hoped he was harassing you?"

"I said I *thought* was harassing me. I said *thought*."

"Ah!" We look at each other for a few seconds, I debating myself as to whether I should begin my interpretation or just keep my nice mouth shut. I keep my mouth shut, smile a pleasant inquisitive smile with my eyebrows up.

"You can't imagine what courage it's taken for me to make that admission."

"I can only imagine, yes."

"I am a very passionate woman."

"Indeed." I nod my head. "I can tell that from the intensity of your writing." This is a slight exaggeration.

"I don't mean writing passionate. I mean sex passionate."

"Ah, yes. Well, they're related, aren't they." Explaining again.

"In my dream—I might as well tell you my latest dream, okay? In my dream we are hugging and kissing passionately." Mrs. Shaw's face is now brilliantly flushed from her forehead down into her brown and yellow neckscarf. She looks only at the table. "I am being bent backwards, like this, and almost smothered, and then suddenly, I can hardly believe it, my husband—ex-husband—shows up. I can see him out of the corner of my eye, over a shoulder, and he just points and laughs." She pauses, not quite panting, looks at me out of the corner of her eye, over a shoulder.

"My! This is very dramatic. I shouldn't wonder you were upset."

"My husband was a rat. Well, enough said about him. He was a rat. Also not much of a man, if you know what I mean." She plucks a tissue from the box, dabs at her forehead and eyes. "Actually, maybe too much of a man, if by man it's somebody who has to do the sex act all the time."

"Some people see that as manly behavior."

"Well, I have a passionate nature, but I cut'n stand that stuff all the time, not that he bothered me a lot."

"You're passionately sexual, but you don't like the sex act."

"Not all the time." She looks at the ceiling. "Actually, I don't like it at all, even though I like the hugging and kissing part, if it's with a nice person. That's the part that's really sexual, y'know, not the other part. The other part is just animal." She gives me a hard look. "Why are you asking me these questions about sex?"

"I, uh, it's something that just happened to arrive in our conversation."

"I personally don't believe what several people said about you."

"Mm-hm." I try to remain unmoved, but I'm quite interested now. Still, I don't ask.

"Aren't you going to ask? Well, what they said was that you have a special fondness for boys, not women. Instead of women, and that's why they fired you. Can you comment on that?"

I almost expect Mrs. Shaw will now delve into her handbag for her fountain pen and notepad, but she only sits expectantly. I do feel a need to respond.

"Mrs. Shaw, I...."

"You should call me Bellona, since we're closer now, almost friends, like, I would say, since I've told you some pretty confidential things."

"Bellona, I retired."

"Everybody says you had to retire or they would have fired you, and they were being generous and nice."

"I retired because they abolished the counseling position and had already abolished the drama program and didn't need me for Spanish, either, because Mr. Peralta can do all of that, now that they've also abolished the school newspaper which he used to do. I understand that several people have suggested that I also have this special fondness for Beauty Jean Dwindle, which I do not. I have a professional interest in Beauty Jean and her little brother."

"The dream wasn't about Jess Pleroma."

"Perhaps you could talk about Jess Pleroma and point out some of those things about him that have caused you to mention his name several times now.

"Well, he's small, but he's wiry-looking, y'know? Quite manly. Lots of curly hair. And he's got an evil reputation." She looks at the table again. "I guess that's one of the things that women find interesting in a man: that he's got an evil reputation. Maybe they want to find out if it's true. That sort of thing. You know."

"An evil reputation is what women find attractive in a man. That's what stimulate the dreams."

"I guess you weren't listening. The dream wasn't about Jess Pleroma at all."

"Oh. Uh-huh."

"But it wut'n do any good, I guess, to tell you who it was."

"Wouldn't do any good?"

"I mean, I look around here and I see you've moved in here. The cot there. The place for clothes. The stuff on the kitchen counter there. So your wife kicked you out because of what you did. Or did professionally. Or dit'n do. Isn't that it?"

I've read about this, the situation wherein the client takes over, kind of like the way Mother Crinkle will do, if you don't watch out. What shall I do? Play the game? I play the game.

"If I tell you, can we then get back to why you came up here in the first place?"

"That's what I been trying to do."

"All right. Of course I've heard the suggestions, but they're the kind of usually vile rumors you hear in Balona about all sorts of people. About me, nobody has ever made a formal accusation that I ever did anything improper with any kid. With anybody, for that matter. And there's a good reason for that."

"What's that?"

"Because it's impossible. I can't do the improper things the rumors call for me doing."

"How's that?"

"I am prohibited. I have a certain, a certain lack of, a lack of ability."

"Ah hah! It's that you are a fine moral man. A man with fine morals." Mrs. Shaw looks a bit disappointed. "Your sense of morality prevents you from committing such offenses. I knew that. I just knew that."

"I'm not excessively moral. I have done some bad things in my life, but not around here, not in this country, and not about sex."

"This is very interesting. Do you know, you get a fine glow to your face when you get excited like this? It makes you look, uh, younger. Did you know that? Maybe you should make yourself get upset more often, Mr. Keyshot, uh, Don."

"About your dreams...."

"They're not about Jess Pleroma at all. They're about you."

Now here's a teachable moment, an opportunity to instruct Mrs. Shaw—Bellona—as to how transference works, and how the therapist becomes the target for all sorts of emotions. My brain has sunk to the pit of my stomach where it begins to growl loudly.

She resumes the initiative. "You're hungry. Can I step over to the sink there and look for some sandwich makings for us? And now that your wife and you are split up, you'll need someplace to go for Thanksgiving turkey, won't you! I know just the place."

Bellona Shaw, passionately sexual or not, is taking over, like Mitzi. It doesn't feel all that bad.

Chapter Fifteen

It has happened without my doing anything, without even hoping. Is that to be the story of my life? I am invited to have my Thanksgiving Dinner with Bellona Shaw, and she is coming to pick me up. I feel almost the way I felt waiting for Mitzi at Frank's Soupe de Jour those long, long months ago, kind of first-datish.

As a young man I never had a first date—or in fact any date—being one of those youngsters who got a job and worked right away, mine being in the basement of an A&P Market, pulling merchandise out of storage, pushing the loaded cart up the ramp to the main floor, and stocking shelves after school and at night.

If Dad didn't borrow my meager pay to accommodate his bookie or his overdue bar bill, Mom would get most of it for her bookie and her overdue bar bill. I don't recall ever objecting, instead feeling proud that I was contributing to family welfare—and hopeful that everything would "get better." Always hopeful.

Dad and Mom didn't live long, not even through my Marine Corps boot camp time, during which I was granted compassionate leave to attend their funeral and settle what was left of their estate. I have never wagered, nor have I indulged in alcohol, except for the occasional Valley Brew.

Balona doesn't seem to have any bookies, but I wouldn't be attracted if it had.

"We might be late if you don't hurry in there, Don. I do have a reservation." Bellona's cheery hail at my door is in a voice much higher on the musical scale than Mitzi's, higher and somewhat louder, as if I were hard of hearing. Alma (ex-Mrs. Peterbilt) Kuhl has a voice like that, possibly cultivated as a result of Alma's need to be heard over the keyboarding and conversations of her students at Balona High. Mrs. Applehanger also has a similar vocal production, possibly affected by her bird-call practice.

Recently I have come to notice that people often shout directions and explanations at those with obvious head injuries, much as they do in response to the queries of foreigners, the reasoning apparently being that more of the same, only louder, should penetrate even the thickest bandaged or foreign skull. The argument is certainly common sense, except that shouting at me, a person with truly superior hearing, only makes my head ache.

Nim Chaud reminded his flock a few weeks ago that common sense is what informs us that the world is flat. He chuckled after reciting that truth and appeared somewhat surprised that some of his listeners had never considered it.

"See, I'm wearing heels." Bellona lifts and straightens her leg, points her foot at my sink, turning the shoe this way and that. "It's actually blue, not black, only it looks black, dut'n it?" Her eyes widen. "You're wearing a necktie. I don't think I've ever seen you with a necktie. It's very debonair. Sort of complements your bandage."

I choose not to contest the observation, although I've always been one of the rare men in Balona who wears a necktie at almost every opportunity.

Her attitude and behavior have become very familiar very quickly.

"Where are we off to?"

"It's a big surprise, but like I said, I've made reservations, so we need to get there on time or they'll have somebody else in our place and take our turkey."

117

The word reminds me of Dirk and I smile ironically, considering how people seem so ready and willing to believe almost anything that degrades someone else.

"Don't forget your cane! We wut'n want you falling down in the street."

I grab my cane from its resting place behind the door. "It doesn't match my attire," I joke. "Should be an ashplant or malacca, not aluminum."

"It seems serviceable enough." Bellona hasn't grasped my humor or my literary allusions.

"Do you like my car?"

"It's very nice."

"It's a Buick, y'know. Bought it new here in Balona this year at Pezmyer's." She nods at Pezmyer's as we pass, closed and dark for the holiday, its electric-blue plastic pennants sagging in the still, moist air. "I like Buicks."

"I like Buicks, too." I feel agreeable today. Besides, my parents and siblings perished in a Volkswagen.

We take the Airport Way route to Delta City, passing Mello Fello. "Not a pizza Thanksgiving?" I am joshing again. She doesn't respond, her eyes firmly on the road, her lips tight. Maybe she's upset about something.

"I notice you dit'n remark on my gown."

"It's very nice."

"I got it special for the occasion. At Runcible's in the Mall."

"Yes, it's very, *very* nice."

"Many men don't notice what women wear."

"Some are more ready to compliment, I guess. I apologize. I should have noticed right away and said something."

"Well, that would be the polite thing to do."

"I see." She made a point of mentioning my necktie. Now she is teaching me how to behave with a grown-up woman.

"Well, you've noticed now, so everything's all right!" She turns her head briefly and smiles the exclamation point. "I've been writing a series—not published yet, of course—a series for the *Courier* about how Balona men don't seem to notice what women wear, or at least don't say anything about it to them. And I think that's what makes women feel unappreciated, y'know? We are always trying so hard to be appreciated, and then our efforts are not even appreciated."

"I appreciate them."

"Well, I mean in general."

"I appreciate them in general, too." I am trying hard to be agreeable, but the conversation seems to be going nowhere. "It may rain again, d'you think?"

"I suppose so. Feels like it. Looks like it. Sort of wet-looking already."

I think about Lamont, dry and snug in his pillow-box. Lamont I appreciate more and more. He has accommodated to apartment living very quickly, using a litter-filled plastic tub for his personal hygiene needs, like a cat. Mr. D.H. Carp scoffed at the possiblity I proposed when I bought the tray and the litter.

"You shut'n have a dog up there in the first place. You'll never get a dog to do his thing in that contraption. That's a cat contraption. Dogs got to go over to the park there." He wrinkled his nose. "Or on my sidewalk." Lamont has defied the odds again. Of course I still need to let him out occasionally to relieve his tensions, but in that respect he does far better than I.

I wish I were sitting in my chair again, right now, dry and snug, reading an engaging book, listening to Tchaikovsky, Lamont snoring snug in his pillow-box beside me. "It is sort of damp looking at that."

"See, now you could express interest in my new feature."

"Another feature? What feature's that?"

"The one I just mentioned. The columns I've been writing. I just said about? About how men never respond to women's needs?"

"Oh. Well. I just thought if you wanted to, you would talk about it."

"We women sometimes need to be encouraged. Especially those of us who have been wounded."

"I see."

"As a psychologist, I thought you might be more sensitive to such needs. But maybe you've never been wounded."

"Never been wounded. I guess not. I'll try harder."

"Of course, Mitzi Crinkle maybe *sort* of wounded you, or you and I wut'n be going to Thanksgiving dinner together, and instead you'd be over at her house with her and Billa Runcible Crinkle." Bellona continues to keep her eyes on the road. She seems to be smiling.

"Mitzi has her own agenda."

"What does that mean, 'own agenda'?"

"It means Mitzi decides what Mitzi wants to do, and then goes ahead and does it. Mitzi is a New Woman, she says, and New Women do that, she says. Who am I to argue with a New Woman."

"Well, I think I'm a New Woman, too."

"Oh. Well, I'm not arguing that, either. I'm a compliant guy. Ah! We're at the Stilton. We're going to the Stilton for Thanksgiving Dinner! I'm impressed." The Stilton Hotel dining room is known for its excellent cuisine. A whole lot better than Frank's; even better than Thanksgiving with, say, Nim Chaud and his tofuburgers and watercress, my uninvited but likely alternative experience for the day. I am delighted at the prospect of Stilton food and must sound so, for Bellona is cheerful again.

"You do have one very endearing feature, though."

She's caught my interest. I cannot let that pass.

"What one very endearing feature is that?"

"It's that you don't argue. I mean, I've been nattering on about all kinds of things—quite personal, in fact—and you haven't talked back even once." She stretches her neck to see herself in the rear-view mirror, brushes her hair back on both sides. "See, I've been testing you!"

"Aha! I thought there was some method there. Did I pass?"

"Well, we'll see. Are you going to open the door for me?"

"Very good. The New Woman will have the Buick's door opened by the Old Man."

"Well, there's such a thing as old-fashioned courtesy, and I'm a person born and bred in the South, where such things matter."

I think about Tara and Scarlet and Rhett, ponder the appropriate Southern Saying, but the moment passes.

The Stilton's atrium has been called Delta City Chic. Some wags have suggested that, except for the elevators crawling up the walls like rose-colored scarabs almost to the glass ceiling that arches eight storeys overhead, the atrium wall with its balconied rows of rooms is said to be reminiscent of the Grand Tier at San Quentin. Perhaps the new apple-green paint job stimulates the prison comparison.

"They have a roof garden up there, too, y'know, over on that side, where Mr. Putzi Purge got murdered. Laid out on the gravel up there. Were you here then?"

"I remained in Balona for those festivities."

"It wat'n festive at all. I was here at the time. It was awful. Poor nice homosexual man. Shot in the head. Nobody knows who did it, even to this day."

"I was being ironic about the festivities."

"Oh, it wat'n ironic at all. Poor man was actually murdered, y'know. Shot in the head. Well, there's Charles. Charles's on duty."

"And has Madam a reservation?" The suave young man demonstrates a slight lisp, is growing a slim mustache to go with his tuxedo. He flutters over both book and Bellona.

"Oh, Charles, we talked on the phone three or four days ago. Bellona Shaw? From the *Courier?* A reservation for two?

"Here it is. Of course, Madam Shaw! This way, please! Watch your step, Mr. Shaw." The solicitous *Maitre d'* Charles seats us at a table in the middle of the room where Bellona can see everyone, everything. "Wolfgang will be your server." Charles tips himself into Bellona confidentially. "Wolfgang is new. It's his first day and, I'm sorry to say, we've had a little difficulty with him since he's sort of European nobility and he sees serving—even in a fine dining room—as a come-down for him. But it's hard to get really competent, experienced servers nowdays, y'know. If everything's not completely satisfactory, please simply signal me, and I will make it right."

Charles snaps his fingers and Wolfgang leaps from where he has been lounging against the wall and presents himself, flapping open our napkins and laying them in our laps, each with a flourish. His cuffs are too long, but not long enough to obscure the tattoo on his right hand: LOVE. I have seen this fellow before, not only in dreams, but on the streets of Balona. Up close he is much slighter than I had thought him to be.

"My goodness!" whispers Bellona. "Do you know who our waiter is?"

This is not Wolfgang, a European aristocrat down on his luck and serving tables at the Stilton. This is Jess Pleroma.

"My good lady," responds the counterfeit Wolfgang, in juicy accents featuring the uvula, "Ish bin, y'know, like, Wolfgang von Pleroma, down on my luck, so you probably think I am lookink like, y'know, mein famous cousin Jess Pleroma of over in Balona, that place, but, like, it iss not. It iss, y'know, like, der Wolfgang here." Wolfgang concludes his introduction with a nice authentic bow and hiss. "At your service!"

He passes a remark with a view to my bandaged head: "Iss a Mahometan holiday, too, yah?"

Der Wolfgang offers appropriate menus while his dark eyes and white teeth flash around a blushing Bellona Shaw. The young man has style. His collar is dirty. His black bowtie is clipped-on crooked. His too-large trousers are bunched under his belt, and he is wearing running shoes instead of patent leather. But he moves gracefully and apes wonderfully the manner of a good waiter. Bellona does the ordering, the standard Stilton Thanksgiving Feast with a nice California champagne.

The courses are served well, are complimented appropriately by the guest as they arrive and as they are consumed. The hostess is a hearty eater and ardent conversationalist, exclaiming over the table decorations of turkey feathers and small pumpkins, also making written notes as to which local celebrities are present, surely recorded for her winningly-titled column, "Beating the Bushes with Bellona of Balona," not political excoriations, but social news. She ignores the waiter appropriately.

Der Wolfgang tops off the flutes without comment but with intense glances for Bellona. I can easily see the attraction. She is a handsome woman with a steady income and a new Buick. Wolfgang flits to serve at other tables.

"I dit'n know he was working here, honestly."

"Does a pretty good job. I had heard that he was almost completely incompetent, except in extracting good automobiles from lonely ladies."

"Do you suppose he learned about me going to be here today and signed on to harass me?"

"It's an interesting idea, perhaps the subject of a column or two?" The temptation to tease is too great. Bellona's eyebrows go up. Her lips make an O. "My! What an interesting idear: Men who set out to seek jobs where they can harass women."

"The food is good, if fateful." I am forking sitzmarks in the whipped cream atop my pumpkin pie, wondering about the actual condition of my arteries. They say that even during the teen years one's arteries begin to harden; that is, begin to accumulate plaques that gradually fill up those channels and eventually cause one's memory and organs to falter and fail. But I am feeling so lively, so cheerful, so hopeful.

"Oh, my! Is this who I think it is?" Bellona's sound is urgent and her face has faded from rose to alabaster. I look back over my shoulder, cholesterol-laden fork in mid-passage.

"I heard he was over here with you. I wut'n believe it. You can't get a man of your own? You gotta take over somebody else's husband for your recreation? You home wrecker!"

This is Mitzi, standing behind me in her spotted yellow fake-fur coat, addressing Bellona not in her usually alto, honeyed television voice. Conversation throughout the entire room has ceased. Earlier one could hear over the sounds of dining the occasional faint shout or clanging noise from the kitchen; these also now cease. Kitchen staff quickly appear, stand along the wall observing the scene.

Bellona Shaw's complexion is dark red now, her eyes rolling like a sheep being dragged onto King Korndog's killing-floor. Raising her napkin she covers much of her face.

I feel like doing the same.

I save the situation with a clever remark. "Hey, Mitzi! How's things? Y'know I never got a Thanksgiving invitation from you—or a visit in the hospital, either."

"You, you, you jerk!" She's ignores my petulant hospital remark. "You're legally my husband. You're supposed to have Thanksgiving at my house."

"We're separated, Mitzi, and in what might be called unfavorable circumstances. I believe that under such conditions a person might celebrate Thanksgiving anywhere he chooses." I hear applause and male exclamations of "all *right!*" from several quarters of the room, quickly followed by shushing sounds, probably female.

"You owe me. I took you in when you needed looking after." She stands back, hands on hips, and glares at me. She has suddenly grown a definite wrinkle, a vertical wrinkle, between the eyes. "We were waiting you. That damn turkey's done. Out of the oven. Getting cold by now. So, are you coming back home with me or not?" Stilton dining is suspended. The entire room awaits my response.

I enunciate clearly, "It is your home, Mitzi, not mine, as you have so frequently mentioned, so of course I am not returning with you."

"Oh. Well, all right for you!" She turns and sweeps out, in the process her fur sleeve knocking glassware off the edge of a nearby table. The party at another table abandon their obvious readiness to applaud the show. All eyes follow Mitzi's departure.

Charles follows as well, shouting in a refined supervisorial way, discreetly, "Wolfgang! Wolfgang boy! Where are you going?"

I am wondering when Mitzi returned to Balona. I am wondering how Mitzi heard I was here.

Wolfgang disappears from the dining room, his napkin and winelist abandoned as he departs. He is following Mitzi. I can only hope for him good luck.

Chapter Sixteen

Lamont evidently is not a practicing bird dog, for he has disdained the leftovers, a good-size box of which Bellona Shaw graciously granted me from our Thanksgiving Feast at the Stilton. Charles outdid himself generosity-wise, possibly from a sense of guilt, possibly out of his awareness of Bellona's potential influence as journalist and commentator on dining and the social life of Chaud (locally pronounced "chawed") County.

I have now for two days enjoyed turkey a la mushroom soup, turkey sandwiches, turkey hash, and turkey with cranberry sauce—breakfast, lunch, and dinner; microwaved turkey, oven-warmed turkey, cold turkey.

I am surfeited on turkey and have at last come to understand how one can have too much of a good thing, a situation I have never before experienced.

Rejection, however, I have experienced aplenty. And now, thanks to me, Mitzi has experienced it once again. Perhaps she is accommodating, for I have seen the Green Giant tooling Front Street under my window several times now. The elbow hanging suavely out of the driver's side is muscular, male, surely Wolfgang von Pleroma's elbow. Whether Wolfgang is in residence at Mitzi's house I do not know. Do I care? Of course I care. She is still my wife. I still love many aspects of her.

But given the multifarious rejections I have experienced at Mitzi's hand, I consider various avenues to dissolving the relationship. I could seek out Kenworth

Burnross, attorney at law, with an office just down the street from here. Mr. Burnross is reputed to be eminently successful with accident cases, particularly those accidents resulting in tragic whiplash injuries.

One may spot on any Balona street a remarkable number of resident Burnross clients limping and hobbling and using canes and crutches, and wearing not only slings and neckbraces, but also kneebraces, anklebraces, backbraces, and elastic bandages. Devices so faithfully exhibited by so many might be taken as evidence of Mr. Burnross's legal bona fides. However, elderly Mr. Burnross has also recently become known on Front Street for showing up at his office sans trousers, young wife Pippa Burnross necessarily bringing the garment to him an hour or more after the beginning of office hours, the pants enfolded in plain brown paper. Everyone knows.

My other candidate for personal legal service provider, Judge Kosh Chaud, is older than Mr. Kenworth Burnross, but Judge Chaud appears to be in full control of his faculties. Perhaps I shall seek his advice and/or legal counsel. Of course, he's Mitzi's lawyer, which might complicate things. In the meantime, someone may be seeking my own counsel, for I hear a great clumping on the stairs and now a knocking at my chamber door.

"It's me, Mr. Keyshot. Joe Kuhl, Private Eye?"

"Come right in, Joseph."

Joe is appropriately dressed this Saturday afternoon: Levi's, a blue long-sleeve polo shirt, and a green apron, the apron being the special garb of laborers at Mr. D.H. Carp's Groceries & Sundries down below my apartment where Joe is sort-of laboring at his part-time job—*sort-of laboring,* in the frequent publicly uttered descriptive phrase of Mr. D.H. Carp.

"I got maybe some news about your attacker, Mr. Keyshot. What I mean is, the guy who probably konked you on the head. Hey, you finally got rid of your Arab hat."

"Sitting right over there on the end of the kitchen counter." I don't correct Joe's ethnic misperception. "You have been hard at work on my case, have you?"

"Night and day, sure. What I mean is, when I'm not slaving away over the books or writing poems or downstairs here, I been lurking in disguise around your house. Watching, y'know? And it's paid off, you'll be happy to know—all that time I been spending. Wanna know what I discovered?"

"Sure do."

"Somebody else is driving your wife's car." He raises one eyebrow and squints his eyes. Both eyebrows now rise, destroying the squint. "It's not the girls' gym teacher, either, the one works out, y'know." The eyes squint again.

"I'm still breathless to know, Joseph."

"It's that scummy Jess Pleroma, that's who." Joe has seated himself in my counselor's chair. Now he leans back and puts his feet on my coffee table, arms folded behind his head, green apron askew. "So now I told you some news about the investigation, maybe you'll give me some advice, like."

"I don't ordinarily give advice, Joseph. What I do is listen to a person, then help him or her figure out the best solution to the problem, et cetera."

"Oh. Well, that's okay, too.

"So?"

"So, well, uh, I got this friend, y'know?"

"It's best when we level with each other, Joseph. You tell it straight and I respond the same way."

"Yeh, so, that's what I'm doing. Like, I got this friend who I like, only she dut'n pay all that much attention to me liking her."

"Ah. What I hear you saying is that you have a friend who seems to ignore your romantic feelings."

"So, like, that's about what I just said. What I mean is, what do I do to make her like me?" He smites his forehead. "What a dumb question to ask. I already know the answer, so why am I asking such a dumb question."

"No such thing as a dumb question, Joseph. Only maybe dumb answers? And I haven't answered yet." I chuckle, show my teeth.

"So?"

I get an inspiration. "You go down the street to the Balona Library and ask Ms Birdie Swainhamer for a book titled *How to Win Friends and Influence People.*"

Joe nods, semi-smiles, his lip lifting ironically.

"You know this book?"

"Hey, how'd you think I got so suave already? I read this book when I was fifteen. You wanna know who recommended it? You wut'n believe it. It was Jess Pleroma, when he was living in our basement. He recommended it. Used to carry it around with him when he wat'n pushing his Bible. He did Bible, too, y'know. Scam, of course."

"My goodness."

"Actually I only read the first 10 pages or so. Not the Bible, the *Win Friends.* Light was bad and I had a lot of homework and headaches just about every day, y'know. What I mean is, the type was small in the book, so you had to hold it sort of close to your eyes, and that made me look like I was going blind. Actually felt like it, too, y'know. So I never actually got around to finishing it."

"Well, if Jess Pleroma recommended it—do you believe that the book helped him at winning friends and influencing people, made him successful at it?"

"Well, he influenced A'nty Pring Chaud, my Cousin Nim's big sister and her Mercedes. And he influenced Francie June Furbeloe and her new Mustang. And my sister Ginger and her Jeep." Joe suddenly turns bright red. "And my ma." He sighs and pales. "Also, he seems to be winning friends with your missus. Yeh, you could say he was successful at it. And I'm s'posed to read this book. And that's your advice is all?"

"The book, old as it is, has a lot of good pointers for just the kind of thing you need. Better than I could say it."

"You're s'posed to be the psychologist, but."

"A counselor, Joseph, with lots of experience with the success of this particular book—and a few others like it."

"I been spending a lot of time, what I mean is: lurking...."

"It's appreciated."

"So, you gonna do something about the guy?"

"We don't know that he was my attacker, do we?"

"Well, he's over there a lot. Hanging around. Driving that neat green Jag a lot. It's a whole lot better than Sammy Joe Sly's Jag, y'know. Dut'n seem to *chug* at all."

I don't ask if Jess Pleroma is actually inhabiting Mitzi's house.

"He's also there late at night. Also early in the morning, says Patella." Patella Sackworth is Joe's classmate who delivers the *Courier*. "She's seen him scratching himself out on your front porch in his bare chest, even in the cold, before the sun comes up—that early. Patella thinks he's cute, she says. What I mean is, I'm sort of embarrassed to mention this, y'know."

Joe is sitting hunched over now, not expansive at all.

"Well, Joseph, all is not as bleak as you might think." I am considering Jess-Wolfgang contemplating Ab Crinkle, and being contemplated in return.

"Well, it sure looks blink to me. But anyways, you're the client. Right?"

"I am still wondering who whacked me."

"Well. There he is, scratching himself. Go figger."

There is a knocking at the door. Surprising, as we have heard no clomping on the stairs. Even Lamont doesn't awaken. "Come on in," I shout.

Bellona Shaw peeps in cautiously. "I wut've called on the phone, but I thought you might be busy up here, so I decided to drop in instead, see how you're doing."

"Other than continuing to burp *molto* turkey, I'm just fine, Bellona. Do you know Joseph Oliver Kuhl?" Joe leaps to his feet.

"Of course I know Joseph. Joseph is maybe going to become a famous columnist at the *Courier*, aren't you Joseph?"

"If I ever get a chance where somebody dut'n always write my column over so nobody reconizes what I wrote in the first place."

"Well, that's editorial privilege, y'know. An editor can just go ahead and re-write. I myself have been re-written, and I am a long-time professional, y'know." Bellona settles herself in my chair; Joe is now seated in the client's chair. I stand at the sink.

"Oh, you sweet doggy!" Bellona reaches over and scratches behind Lamont's ears. Lamont smiles, returns to his nap.

"I suppose you've been talking about the latest news." Bellona's color is especially high, her eyes are shining, she looks more appealing than when she's being New Woman, complaining and being commanding.

I smooth my eyebrows, which have a tendency to flare. "Joseph has been talking about his investigative practice, and I've been listening and learning." Joe glows.

"I mean the news about the latest assault."

"What assault?" Joe sits forward, ears up.

"Another victim was found in your azaleas today, Don. Dit'n you know? Nobody called you up and told you? Of course, they *are* Mitzi Crinkle's azaleas."

"What victim?"

"Well, Joseph, they found that young rascal, that Jess Pleroma, head down in Mr. Keyshot's front porch bushes, same way they found Mr. Keyshot last week. Young Jess is over at Doctors Hospital right now, I heard, getting bandaged up. Apparently got whacked pretty hard with a blunt instrument."

I look at Joseph whose eyes are squinted, perhaps in puzzlement.

"Another blunt force, of course," he mutters. He turns his attention to me. "Do you s'pose it could be Patella does it? She's around all over downtown Balona early every morning, and she's not as strong as my ma, but I bet she's strong anyways. I never even thought it could be Patella, but it could be. I better go investigate."

"Well, you two handsome young men, I have to be off now, too, and write up the story so I don't miss my deadline. I just wanted to make sure you'd heard about it, since you are so, so, connected, you might say." She gives me an eyes-narrowed look so that I know I may now be a suspect in this latest assault. "Do you have any comment, Mr. Keyshot?"

I look blank. I think blank.

"I bet the *Beacon* would buy my story." Bellona is gone even before Joe.

Chapter Seventeen

The wheeze and spoonerisms are unmistakable. "We got us a pine on the lerp that konked you, Mr. Keyshot. So—not that it's gonna make a whole lot of difference—when you're beeling fetter, come on across the street and let's cav a honfab. I got young Joey Kuhl here, since he says he's working for you. That right?" I confirm Constable Lafcadio Hearn Gosling's query.

Cod's statistics on solving crimes are not impressive, but then there aren't many crimes that need solving in Balona. Most crimes that surface he can afford to overlook because they are small and overlookable. Most such crimes are committed by city fathers or ex-city fathers or the wives and children of city fathers or other *relatives* of city fathers or ex-city fathers, so it would seem impolitic to roil the civic blend.

Last summer there *may* have been a crime when a city slicker settled in with a scam to bilk citizens in a movie-made-in-Balona scheme. But the slicker perhaps never committed an act that constituted a complete and identifiable crime. Besides, he moved on suddenly. Besides, he was a relative of the town's only pharmacist, a new business at that. Besides, he left Jess Pleroma behind, who ratted on his partner in probable crime and took the jail time in Delta City.

The Balona crimes that are most profitable to town coffers are traffic crimes, and their profitability adheres partially to the Council and partially to the constable. Cod effectively controls Balona's only traffic light, and has achieved such a mastery of the system that he is

133

able to violate the most conscientious driver at will, simply by means of the well-coordinated movement of the officer's thumbs on the electronic controls in his office.

In dry weather Cod spends most of his time on the bench outside his office or in Frank's Soupe de Jour, having one of his frequent diurnal between-meals Franksburgers. Today he's sitting on his bench in the Front Street fog, munching popcorn from a large brown shopping bag. Joe Kuhl is seated beside him, occasionally dipping his hand into the bag. "How's things, Mr. Keyshot? Here, take a handful or two. Plenty here. More inside the office there."

I wag my head slowly. "How's things, Cod? Joe? I thought maybe the sheriff assigned some of his guys to look into the assault."

"Naw. He does that only when I can't pigger the ferp out, and then I give him a call. Y'know. So I figgered I'd give this guy some time and he'd maybe do it again and piv us a gattern for his crimes. Y'know. That's a police crime-busting technique."

"That's right, Mr. Keyshot. What I mean is, Cod's right about that."

"Actually I got more than a line on the perp. I got me a witness."

I gasp. "A witness to my attack?"

"A witness to kess getting jonked."

Joseph interprets: "He means Jess getting konked."

"It was Patella. Patella on her route."

"He means Patella's newspaper delivering. What he means is, she delivers the *Courier* and the *Beacon* both." Joseph's interpreting doesn't seem to bother Cod, but it strikes me much as my explaining must annoy my clients—and my former students and counselees.

"So? Well?" I search each popcorn-masticating face. "You actually mean Patella did it?"

"No, not Patella, not her! Patella *seen* it."

I repeat: "So? Well?"

"You mean 'so, well' like who done it?"

"Yes! Who is it?" I'm almost shouting here.

"You gotta understand it's only Patella, and it was still dark, being early morning, and the batteries on Patella's bike light are sort of weak, and Patella's sort of dramatic inclined, y'know, like she imagines stuff. Like, what I mean is, she imagines I'm her steady boyfriend, which I'm not, y'know." He looks at Cod. "You gonna tell him?"

"I dunno. He'll expect me to do something about it."

"I would indeed. I mean, I *will* expect you to do something about it. I mean, the person who asaulted Jess Pleroma almost undoubtedly assaulted me, put us both in the hospital. Of course I'll expect you to do something about it."

"See what I mean?" This to Joseph.

"Well, Cod, Mr. Keyshot's got a point."

"But, well." Cod thinks, folds the now empty popcorn sack into a quarto, rubs his stomach. "I think I could use a Franksburger and a cuppa." He rises and waddles off. Joe and I follow.

"Nice cane, Mr. Keyshot. Nice and heavy, wut'n you say?"

"Heavy, Joseph?"

"And blunt. A blunt object, wut'n you say?"

Joe seems to be hinting. "Are you trying to tell me something?"

"Um. I'm just maybe, what I mean to say is, maybe I'm sort of hinting, in case Cod don't, dut'n want to let you in on it. What I mean is, it's not provable, except maybe by Patella's testimony—and everybody knows Patella's testimony's complete hooey; it'n worth the paper it's printed on." I believe I can hear intruding into this dialog the not-so-subtle demeaning of a competitor for *Courier* columnist honors. Am I mistaken?

We take seats in the same front booth in which I first entertained Mitzi. I sit in the very same spot I sat on that fateful first date. It is perhaps on this very same table-top grease spot that I have laid my arm. Frank apparently saw Cod coming, for Cod is already chewing away at his Franksburger. Plenty of onions, anyone can tell.

"So, Cod. I am about as discreet a person as you'll ever meet. Besides, I've been a victim—probably—of this perpetrator. So, don't you feel now somewhat justified in sharing some of your deductions?" I'm appealing to the constable's ethics here.

He finishes his burger, burps, raises his eyebrows. "Can you guess?"

"I don't have a clue."

"That's what everybody says about you!" Cod's eyes hardly show their humorous crinkle because of the excess adipose tissue.

"Please!"

"Oh, well, okay. Patella says she seen Jess get whacked by Mitzi's ma, Billa Crinkle. Konked him with her cane. Give him several good ones, and then poked him for good measure while he was laid out in the azaleas there. Then old Billa looked over at Patella and give her a hard look and went back inside, smiling to herself."

"Mother Crinkle?"

Joe: "Well, that's Patella for you. Maybe making stuff up, since she don't, dut'n like Mrs. Crinkle all that much, Mrs. Crinkle making smart remarks and snorting about Patella's oversize body parts, eksedra. Patella also works part-time over at Kute Kurls & Nails, sweeping up, y'know, but really to get the down-and-dirty from the ladies talking."

Cod again: "So, now we got us a sort-of perp, do I go over and arrest the old lady?"

"Well, you have a crime and a witness. Two crimes.

Sure, you arrest the alleged perpetrator. Don't you?"

"No, I don't."

"Would you help me understand how come not?" I use the "help me understand" thing with Cod because it's a favorite counseling line of mine and doesn't seem to get clients upset.

Cod replies: "Billa Crinkle was Billa Kuhl before she was Billa Runcible. She's a Kuhl, Mr. Keyshot."

"She's a relative of mine."

"She's a relative of mine, too, Joey, since me and you are related. But the thing is, you wanna ast, how come the sheriff's guys it'n over here investigating and making arrests?"

"Yes, exactly. So, how come?"

"Well, even though I never ast for 'em, they was. They was both over here, asting questions and looking around. Even went to your house, Mr. Keyshot—your old house, I mean—and talked to your wife or ex-wife or maybe to-be-ex-wife. And Anson told me they had a long interview with your ex-mother-in-law. They figgered out right away who whacked you. That's mainly how come you're off the hook for whacking Jess. Well, so then the sheriff's boys went back to Delta City and reported to the sheriff—and never come back."

"How do you explain that?"

"I ast Sheriff Chaud. I said, 'Anson,' I call the sheriff Anson to his face, y'know, since he's almost my uncle, except not quite. I said, 'Anson, how come you called off yer dogs over here on the Keyshot caper?' And you know what he says? He says, 'Hey, nobody was kilt, and Billa Crinkle's a Kuhl, and I'm not stirring up *that* pot again.' That's exactly what he said: *Billa Crinkles's a Kuhl.*"

"So?"

"So, there you have it. That's why the sheriff dalled off his cogs. No use stirring the pot. No use trying to sweep up spilt milk. Water's under the sink."

"Well, what about the victim?"

"What about it? You got insurance. That's what insurance is for, to take care of life's little problems like
that."

"What about my pain and suffering?"

"What about it? You the only one in the world got
sane and puffering? Nothing new about that! Now, if
she'd used a baseball bat, now that might be some
pain and suffering. But that little cane of hers and she
being 96 years old and all—well, I don't think anybody's gonna put a 96-year-old great-great-grandma in
the pokey. D'you?"

"Well, at least it ought to get on the record."

"No proof. Forget it."

The bell over the door jingles and Patella Sackworth
in her trademark purple sweatsuit enters, her eyes for
Joseph alone. "Hey, Joey! How's things?" Although I
slide over toward the wall, Joe doesn't move to give her
room in the booth, but she slips in and sits part-
perched on the very edge of the bench beside him.

"Hey, yeh, Patella. How's things? You're crowding me
a little here. I gotta have room for my elbow to raise up
my cup."

"Well, so move over a fraction. So how's about me
taking you out to Mello Fello for a nice milkshake? I'm
buying."

"I could get a milkshake right here if I wanted one,
but what I mean is, I'm having a cuppa here with my
client Mr. Keyshot and Cod as you can plainly see, if
you just look."

"Oh, yeh. Hello, Mr. Keyshot. Hello Cod. So how's
things?"

"How's things, Patella?"

Patella lowers her voice slightly. "Frank always, like,
coughs over the ice cream every time he opens up the
freezer so, like, the milkshake hygiene is sort of per-
verted here. Would you actually want a milkshake

that's been coughed all over?" She makes a perverted-milkshake face, adjusts her pink plastic-frame glasses with both hands and looks at my head. "You got your bandage off, so I guess it's all okay. The head I mean."

"I'm healing nicely. I understand you witnessed a similar crime recently."

"Oh, yeh! I saw old Mrs. Crinkle—the old lady, not your wife—smack that cute Jess Pleroma a couple times pretty hard. Lotta steam for an old lady. Yeh, I saw that, right there on your front porch. But I guess you don't live there anymore, I hear."

"You're sure it wasn't somebody else?"

"Oh, no. It was old Mrs. Crinkle, all right. When she finished her whacking, she looked pretty pleased with herself, y'know. It was me called 9-1-1 that sent the ambulance over and picked him up. Called on my cellphone here. Otherwise, the handsome guy'd probably still be there bleeding in the bushes." Patella looks at Joseph and smiles. "I've already written my column about it. Probably win a prize."

"I'm writing a column, too, about how witnesses are so flaky and don't actually see what they think they see, especially in the dark of the morning fog, eksedra. I wut've got my column in this week's *Courier,* but I'm working for a client right now and that keeps me going day and night." Joe slurps at his coffee, makes a face, puts more sugar in the brew and clanks his spoon, stirring vigorously.

"Patella, are you willing to swear to what you saw?"

"For what? Why would I swear?"

"I mean, if I were to prefer charges."

"Oh, no, Mr. Keyshot. No, I wut'n."

"Well, you saw the assault and you called 9-1-1 for the victim and you can identify the perpetrator."

"Oh, well, but, like, y'know, this is Balona, and old Mrs. Crinkle is a Kuhl."

⚘
Chapter Eighteen

It's a dream I haven't had since the better years of my childhood. I recognize it at once as my Comfortable Dream, although it does have some rough and puzzling edges. I relax into it.

My mother is leaning over me, pulling the covers up to my chin, over my arms. I resist. "I'm fine. I'm fine," I say, "Don't worry," pushing the covers down to my chest again. I am perhaps nine years old, of course lying in my bed on the back porch where I slept summer and winter; my small brother and sister occupied the second of the two bedrooms. My mother's breath is laden with whiskey and cough drops. Her eyes are glowing, wet brown.

"I'm sorry, Donny. I'm so sorry." She says the words again and again and continues trying to pull the covers up to my chin, tuck me in. Her tears drip onto my face.

"It's okay. I'm fine. It's okay. I'm fine."

This is my Comfortable Dream. She doesn't say she loves me. She doesn't hug me or kiss me. She never hugs me or kisses me. She only tells me she's sorry. Sorry about what, I don't know, but the words and the tears are comforting—because they are for me alone. And I know she loves me.

Of course I at once traipse down to Tabernacle, describe the reappearance of my comfortable dream to Nim in the middle of the afternoon when I should be manning the phone in my office, waiting for clients to call. "Mother never hugged or kissed me, but this dream is a comfortable change, don't you think?"

"Interesting. Yes, it sounds affirmative. My mother never hugged me or kissed me, either." This is the first time I can remember that Nim has mentioned his mother or shared anything of a family nature. "But I know she loved me. There are many ways to express love beside hugging and kissing, aren't there. Matter of fact, hugging and kissing may be substitutes for real love, right? She made shirts for me. She washed my clothes. She was always cooking and baking and having me try out her special recipes. She looked at me with a kindly, loving expression on her face. She was pained when I hurt myself. Yes, she loved me. She sent me packages of food and socks and a fine scarf when I was overseas. She was just not physically demonstrative."

He nods his head and laughs gently at this, at the remembrance of his mother knitting a thick wool scarf for a marine fighting a war in tropical jungles. "Remember that blue scarf, Keyhole? I wore it sometimes and occasionally found it useful, if not always necessary to keep off Jack Frost!" His voice softens. "Yes, she loved me." He looks at me. "Your dream expresses hope as well as love, hope that all will be well., doesn't it. Tucking you in like that is an expression of love."

"I guess so. I feel better after I experience it. I'm feeling better right now, just from talking about it."

"It's the thing with feathers again."

"What about him?" I'm puzzled about Nim's sudden reference to the eminently respected hospital corpsman whose skills saved our lives so many years ago.

"Do your remember your poetry? Emily Dickinson?" He recites in his beautiful bass-baritone:

> "Hope is the thing with feathers
> that perches in the soul
> and sings the tunes without the words
> and never stops at all."

"Yes, it's 'the thing with feathers, without the words,' now I remember. Yes. Well, it's still there, isn't it, even though in my case 'Thing' seems to have laid off singing once in a while—maybe to catch a breath!"

"You're looking hopeful, Don. Your posture is more erect. Your color is higher, your eyes brighter. I'll bet your appetite is keener. What do you suppose is stimulating all this positive energy?"

"I've been trying to put Mother Crinkle out of my mind. I think it surely must have been she who left that 'wimp' note for me where I'd find it. Well, she's justified in a way."

"How can you say that?"

"She wants Mitzi to have babies. She believes I'm the one who held that up. Told me as much. When you get right down to it—even though she doesn't really have the information and doesn't figure-in Mitzi's proclivities—she's right. I could never participate in her formula for success. Well, she better than most can see the Dark Angel's approach, and she doesn't want her dynasty to end with Mitzi barren. Of course, Mother Crinkle had six or seven other kids long before Mitzi, each producing a squad of grandchildren and now great-grandchildren."

"Penny Preene has nice things to say about you."

"About me? Penny Preene?"

"Yes, indeed. She mentioned how helpful you were in getting Claire her scholarship."

"Oh, well."

"Bellona Shaw has nice things to say about you."

"Has she!"

"Yes, about how Old World Gallant you are, and how that courteous nature has even rubbed off onto your dog, and about how handsome you have suddenly become—now that you're on your own, she says." Nim is smiling broadly. "I think maybe she's in love."

I feel myself coloring. "She's a nice person, but I can't

get involved that way again, Nim. It's too, you know."

"I *don't* know, Don. I'm just reminded of the words of—who was it? Oscar Wilde? who said, *When you really want love, you will find it waiting for you.* It seems to me that you have what any thinking woman would give the world to have in her man: a loving nature, intelligence, a profession, kindness and courtesy, and a reasonably good retirement income."

"Not to speak of an unwholesome reputation."

"That's nonsense. Anyone who knows you knows it's nonsense."

"Well, I may not be lacking in what any thinking woman wants, but I have a hell of a lot lacking in what a flesh-and-blood woman needs."

Nim blushes, but wags his head. "No, from what I have learned in my reading and counseling, I can say that ingenuity and love will overcome. I should remind you—and I've not reminded many people—I was once married myself, a very long time ago."

"I respect your opinion, Nim, but may I remind you of something I've reminded few others: I have to take shots to make sure I speak in a normal voice. I have nothing down here to satisfy a woman with. This marine has to sit down to pee, man. Lamont watches me on the pot. I can see pity in his eyes. Lamont can aim and whiz at a fireplug or a tree or a post. Even he has that satisfaction." The comfortable remainder from my dream is slipping away.

"The plastic surgeons could have helped you out there."

"I told them to go to hell. I was sick of the pain and fearful of the kind of life I was sure to have, even with more surgery. Frankly, I wasn't planning on staying alive."

"I recognize those feelings, but there are new remedies available, I'm sure; at least partial remedies."

"No longer interested, Nim."

"Well, I'll say it again: ingenuity and mutual respect and love can overcome."

"I told Mitzi, y'know, beforehand. The deal with her was supposed to be a mutual benefit arrangement, y'know, but with considerable regard on my part for her. I was prepared to enter our partnership with ingenuity—sexual ingenuity and creativity, to put it bluntly. She said my problem didn't matter as she wasn't interested in sex in any way, shape, or form. That wasn't at all true, but it hardly matters now. Unfortunately, I didn't want to believe her when she went on about her aversion. I figured my loving her could *cure* her. How about that! Anyway, it doesn't matter."

"Don, it matters now for your future happiness as much as it ever mattered, and as much as it ever will matter. I'll say it once again: ingenuity and mutual respect and love can overcome."

As usual, when I left Nim Chaud I was feeling good, if not perfect. I'm boiling an egg, feeling almost cheerful, when comes the knock on the door.

"Come on in," I sing.

"I was shopping downstairs and I saw your sign on the building there and I thought, well, I thought I'd pop up and say hello."

It's Penny Preene, probably the most beautiful woman in Chaud County, daughter of the late alleged sex-fiend Pastor Pius Preene, probably the most beloved and vilified man in Chaud County in his time. Penny is the mother of Claire Preene, who is probably the richest young woman in Chaud County as a result of her being the natural daughter and heir of Oliver Kuhl, who indulged his penchant for innocent, lonely, needful, beautiful young girls.

"Come right in, Ms Preene! Have a seat there while I turn off my egg and let it simmer."

"I'm interrupting your lunch."

"You're here just in time to help me watch my egg cool. When it's all cooled I'll mash it up on a piece of bread with some mayonnaise and some lettuce and make me a sandwich. But that's for later. I cannot successfully mash up a hot egg. Not that skilled."

"Claire said you have a sense of humor!"

"She's doing well, I'll bet."

"She wants to play the flute professionally, so she's studying hard."

"Sounds successful already." Penny is wearing her bright red hair down and pulled back in a pony tail. Without makeup her unlined face and open gaze render her about 18 years old.

"Mmm. Smells good in here. What is that?"

"Well, if it isn't essence of lavender on Lamont there, it's probably the incense Nim Chaud used to burn when he lived here. Sandalwood, I think. Soaked into the walls, I guess. So, how can I help you?"

"Well, I saw your sign down there."

"Just screwed it on last week."

"You're taking clients."

"As fast as they can make it up those stairs." I sit and we look at each other.

"Thank you for helping Claire so much."

"My pleasure. She's a wonderfully bright, thoughtful, caring young woman."

"I thought maybe I could ask you some stuff about something else."

"About Claire?"

"Well, about another girl, a sort-of friend of Claire's."

"A sort-of friend."

"I know that sounds strange, but the friendship is strange. The friend is from a females-only Vietnamese refugee family; all the males dead. She's very friendly but she's not at all outgoing about personal things, and Claire has been trying for years to melt her a little. If I get her to come up here, would you talk to her?"

145

"Is there a problem?"

"She has ambitions but she has family problems and she's poor. And I have the feeling she's not well."

"I don't know what I could do for her. She must be the young woman who would never show up for counseling when she had the opportunity back at Balona High."

"I think there were reasons. Would you do it?"

"Sure. I'll try." I hope I am not revealing to this compassionate woman my reticence, my concern—say it—my fear. Balona is an insular community where I've been for a long time. I've tried not to think about Vietnam or Vietnamese. To do so now will take some doing. "So, what else?"

"About me."

"About you? Wouldn't Pastor Nim do the far better job?"

"He's maybe too close. I mean, he knows me so well I'm afraid he'd just laugh and say 'no problem,' the way he often will when people present him with dumb problems." She makes a slight *moue*. "Actually, he sort of said you would be better than him with this thing I've got. It's Pastor Nim who's referred me to you."

"Well, all right! So you are looking to me for professional help, as they say?"

"I can pay. And I will pay for the girl I mentioned."

"Good. I was worried that maybe you were going to run off leaving me penniless." We laugh. "Sure, talk away."

She spends several minutes speaking of peripheral things, as clients are wont to do. I respond according to form, pleasantly.

"I'd like to get married."

"Yes."

"I've never been married."

"I see."

"Yes. I'd like to get married now, but I don't know

146

how to go about it."

"Well. You now have a friend with whom you're involved?"

"Of course. Everybody in town knows I'm involved with Mark. You've seen us together any number of times. He's come to every one of Claire's recitals. We go all sorts of places together. I worked on his school board campaign which, by the way, he won, y'know."

"Yes, I voted for him. Well?"

"I love him so. I'd like to marry him."

"Yes."

"He hasn't asked me. He's never kissed me. He looks at me, y'know, but he never kisses me or even hugs me."

"Ah." Hugging and kissing again. On the tube even strangers who have never been introduced leap into the sack together and make passionate love for everyone to witness. In Balona these two beautiful people are seen together everywhere, but in fact they place themselves at arms length from each other.

"I think he may still be in love with Elaine, his wife. Maybe you remember her? A lovely person. My friend. She died five or six years ago."

"Whenever I have seen you and Mark together, his expression and his attentiveness tell everyone that he's devoted to you."

"Does he? Does he really? Yes, of course, he does. I know that. But still...."

"So, how do you intend to solve the problem?"

"Well, I don't know. I thought that maybe you could help. I mean, tell me what to do."

"I can't tell you what to do. What I can do is make a suggestion. Tell him. Okay?"

"Tell him? Oh, my!" Her voice is low, her expression is worried.

"Tell him. You could rehearse it, make up a script and recite it. For example, you could say, 'Mark, I love you and would like to marry you. Would you marry me?'"

"Oh, I cut'n say that." Her deep brown eyes are closed.

"Why not?"

"Well. I don't know."

"That's my suggestion. Maybe you could try it."

"My goodness. Is that all there is to it, d'you think?"

"That's all there is to lots of problems we think are complicated."

"I could say, 'Mark, I love you. Will you marry me?' I could say it just like that. And if he says no...."

"Then you can start over again." I smile. I cannot imagine Mark Ordway refusing this rare and wonderful creature.

"Oh, my! Oh, my! I wonder if I went over to the *Courier* and saw him there, if I could ask it there? No, I probably should do it at the house when he comes over for dinner. He's coming over for dinner tonight. Yes, I'll do it tonight. He'll be surprised, won't he?"

She rises, her face flushed, her eyes shining. "I'm so glad I came up here. It was on the thought of a moment, y'know, that I actually walked up those stairs. I saw that sign and I remembered what Pastor Nim said, but I never thought I'd 'seek counseling,' like they say on the TV. But here I went and did it. Ah! I'm so proud of myself. Oh, what do I do about paying you?"

"I send you a bill, and you write me a check."

"Simple as that. Oh, I'm so glad I came up here. The girl's name is Thuy Le, remember?" She takes my hand and wrings it. As she departs she is talking to herself, perhaps rehearsing her script. I have a feeling she won't need more than the first clause.

I hear her voice on the stairs. "Oh, hello Miss Crinkle!" I don't hear the response, but Mitzi pops right in without knocking.

"I see you've started on another one right away, the

first one not even cool yet."

"What?"

"The redheaded widow down there, the one without a brassiere. She in your harem now along with that old cow from the *Courier*? I must say you move fast. Got your tongue in shape, have you? Better have."

"I...."

"Well, here." She hands me an envelope, takes out a comb and works on her hair. "You sign this and return it in the mail, and afterwards you wait a while—and that's the end of our stupid marriage. I'm sorry you weren't able to live up to your end of the bargain, but that's the way the cookie bounces, I guess. I see you still got that cur. D'you know he gives off an awful smell? Smells like dog and sweat up here."

Mitzi puts her comb away, turns and leaves without another word. On the stairs I hear a loud "Moooooo!" Still Mitzi.

And then at the door it's Bellona Shaw.

"What was that all about, d'you suppose, that mooing?"

"Haven't the slightest idea. Would you like some tea, Bellona?"

"Delighted." She squints her eyes at me, looking me up and down as I prepare the tea. "I saw Miss Crinkle when I was coming up here."

"Mm-hm. Yes, she was delivering some papers."

"Before her, I saw somebody else coming out of your stairway."

"Oh? Oh, yes, indeed. Ms Penny Preene. Yes. Penny Preene." I pause in my tea-making and think about Ms Penny Preene's charms. I wish for discretion's sake that there were a rear exit to this place instead of a single fire escape ladder that ends six feet above Mr. D.H. Carp's dumpster.

"Penny Preene was up here for a while, I guess."

"You yourself are her witness. Yes."

I pour. We stir in our condiments and sip and consider. I suppose I am smiling.

"You're smiling."

"What? Oh, yes. I was just thinking how one's moods can be changed by such simple circumstances. For example, I had a dream."

"Ah. It must've been an erotic dream." Bellona is frowning, perhaps having forgotten the joyful parts of her own erotic dreams.

"No, it was a dream from my childhood, and it has brought back many good feelings. It's countered some of my bad dreams."

"And I guess Penny Preene brought up some nice feelings."

"Oh, yes. She's marvelously beautiful, isn't she?" Perhaps that was the wrong thing to say.

"Well, I just dropped in to say hello, so now that I've said it and seen you so happy and victorious, I guess I'll just be on my way." She puts her cup in the saucer with a flourish and a clatter.

"Stay a while and chat, Bellona. You've never finished our interview for your story."

"What story is that?"

"Your feature on Don Keyshot, Counselor?"

"Oh, that. Well, I'm still thinking about that. And right now I've got another couple fish to fry." She packs up and leaves.

I crack open my hard-boiled egg, work on it with a fork, mix it with mayonnaise and a little mustard and grated onion, look for the bread, hum a happy tune without words, not stopping at all.

Chapter Nineteen

"I thought it would be scary to talk to you, Mr. Keyshot. That's why I never answered your notes at school; but, now I'm up here in this place, I find it's not so scary after all." The young woman smiles a very small smile, leans out of her chair to view Lamont, who gazes a response from the comfort of his pillowbox, his tail thwacking pillows in approval. I don't reveal to her that I thought it might be scary for *me* to speak with *her*. "Scary because we're not used to, like, telling people stuff." She sounds like a Balona teenager. Of course, she *is* a Balona teenager.

Lamont is a good judge not only of character, but also of mood, so I ask him: "Lamont, is this young woman comfortable, d'you think?" Lamont responds with a yawn. "Lamont's yawn means the guest could use a cup of tea. Could you use a cup of tea, Thuy?"

Thuy hesitates, looks closely at Lamont, nods her head, smiles. I prepare and serve the tea, Japanese green tea, another gift of Nim Chaud.

Thuy is tiny and small-boned, pale, with a heart-shaped face, dark brown hair, large brown eyes. The paleness predominates. For such a young person she presents as extremely weary. She almost makes a face when she first sips, then probably out of politeness, sips again.

"Different, isn't it."

"Yes, quite different. But I have tasted it before at Jack Ordway's grandma's house, and it's, like, okay, Mr. Keyshot. But I'm not supposed to drink tea."

"It is pretty strong; probably has a lot of caffeine."

"It's okay."

"Names usually mean something. What does *Thuy* mean?"

Her face and neck become dark red and she lowers her face into her cup briefly before she responds. "It means *beautiful one*. Hardly appropriate, but my mother tells me that my father was always hopeful. Some of the kids still pronounce it *thoo-ee* instead of *twee*. Richie Kuhl still hollers *thoo-ee* at me, like it was some kind of disease." She sighs, puts he cup on the table, watches it.

"The name is beautiful however it's pronounced. My mother's name was Rue, which is a kind of flower, I think."

"I thought for a while that I would take an American name, since I'm an American now, not a Vietnamese, and since I've lived here, like, most of my life. When I first got here they put me in the sixth grade, and my principal called me into her office and said I should change my name so I would, like, 'fit in' better, she said. She wanted to name me Margaret or Victoria.

"That was when I was really only a little kid, before I could speak a lot of English. I went home and told my mother they said I had to be called Margaret or Victoria from now on, so I would fit in. But my mom wouldn't hear of it. She was scared to make any objection, but anyway she asked the social worker to tell the principal my name is Thuy. Even so, I'm all-American now. Of course, you'd never know it from looking at me, would you? Or from watching me at home with my mom or my aunties. With them I, like, y'know, speak Vietnamese and still breathe Vietnam."

"Your family came here from Vietnam after the war."

"My family went to Hong Kong after the war, when I was a baby. Had to leave Vietnam because my father was on the wrong side back there and cut'n get work.

We stayed in a camp in Hong Kong for a long time. That's where my father finally died, and my little brother. My big sister died in the boat on the way to Hong Kong and my father was shot then, too, when the pirates came, and I almost didn't make it. But I don't remember any of that." Thuy's tone is conversational.

Her father was "on the wrong side," so I didn't shoot him after all. "And all of you ended up in Balona."

"The church sponsored us. What was left of us."

"Pastor Nim's Tabernacle."

"No, the other church, the one with the big front steps and the porch in front. I don't remember the name. They have a piano, where Tabernacle has an organ. I go over there once in a while to say thanks, but I don't really know anybody there. I do know they're, like, y'know, disappointed that we don't go there regularly and celebrate Christian holidays. All that stuff. We appreciate their kindness and generosity though."

"Well, you're now a high school senior. As I recall you've done well in school."

"After my eighth-grade teacher—Ms Fardel—sat me down and taught me to read, after school, every day, most of a semester. After that, it was easy and I, like, studied night and day. And Claire is my friend. That has helped a lot."

"And what now? You're happy now."

We sit in silence for some minutes, perhaps pondering my last statement. Thuy looks at the carpet, blinks several times slowly before she responds. "It's not polite to complain or make a scene, y'know, right? And even if a person was impolite and complained, even if she had reason to complain, what use is complaining about something that's over with and done? I mean, your life is what's laid out for you—and you live it the best way you can. So I don't think about being happy or being unhappy. I'm glad I'm still alive and I'm hoping to stay alive a while more. A little while maybe." She looks like she could use a hug, but given the community's enthusiam for believing me to be both lecher and bugger, and Thuy's initial statement about being afraid to come up here, I restrain myself.

"So, Ms Penny Preene is your friend, too, I guess, along with Claire."

"Yes, she's nice. She's the one suggested I could talk with you."

I look at her and nod my agreement; she looks everywhere but in my eyes. She has something to say.

"I do have, like, a secret I maybe should tell somebody before it happens."

A secret. I need to restrain not only the urge to hug, but also the impulse to tell her why she's here, explain how counseling works, et cetera.

"I am learning to play the violin."

"Ah! Good. That will bring you lots of good feelings."

"Yes, my mother doesn't object to it, except for the practicing. The squeaks make her nervous. I don't like to make my mom nervous. She's nervous a lot."

"But that's not the secret you came to talk about."

"Oh, no. That's not the secret. Anyways, my mom's always been nervous. She's, like, sick, y'know. Not sick like me. She's got another sickness I can't talk about here."

"But not sick like you."

"No, not like me. Your dog keeps looking at me."

"Lamont is a fine judge of beauty as well as of character. He tells me he thinks you are beautiful." Thuy is beautiful. Maybe I've pushed the envelope out too far with such a remark.

She only smiles. It's a one-sided ironic smile, much as Joseph Kuhl makes when he speaks of his mother and his family's need for counseling. Thuy looks at my chest. "May I speak?"

"Of course, Thuy! I hope that's why you're here—to express some concerns and work out some problems that I may be able to help you with, in my small way."

"It's that I don't feel comfortable complaining, when I've had so many lucky breaks. Like, I'm alive, after all. I shut'n be alive, y'know. I shut've died already."

I can't say anything; I know the feeling intimately and I swallow the lump in my throat. I nod my head. Is it almost as if I'm agreeing that she should have already died? No, it's to encourage her to go on.

"I have dreams about awful things."

Another dreamer. Not like Bellona Shaw's dreams. Not, I hope, like my bad ones. "We can talk about them."

"I don't remember them. I just know they're awful. I wake up crying, with wet tears, like."

"Do you know I have dreams, too. Not pleasant ones, sometimes." I should keep my mouth shut and listen.

"A long time ago I told the doctor at the clinic over in Delta City and he said the dreams may be, like, stimulated by some kind of poison passed on to me when I was born. Like something from the war. And that's what's making my body fall apart."

"I don't understand. Are you saying you have a physical problem?"

"Oh, yes. I'm going to die pretty soon, the doctors think. That's my secret, Mr. Keyshot—not that I play the violin, in case you thought that." She laughs, as if deprecating the importance of her secret. "They say they are amazed I've lived this long. It's something I can't talk about with Claire. Or my mom, either. Or my aunties. I asked the doctors not to tell my mom and my aunties yet. My mom and my aunties have already, like, suffered too much pain." She looks at Lamont again. "So I thought maybe if I talked with you, you could sort of tell me what to do, how to let them know, like, without making them hurt too much, y'know? That's what a counselor does, it'n it? Tells you what to do about your problems?"

I explain and over-explain about the counseling process, as is my bent. She nods, probably understands, needs to talk.

"My mom and my aunties, they want to see me married pretty soon and happy and having babies. They want to see me making the family alive again. They have a lot of hope for me. But all of that's not going to happen." She takes a breath, spasmodically, and her lips tighten, as if to hold in a sob. "So something happened to me because of the war over there. I can never marry. I can never have babies. I can't make the family alive again. The family ends with me."

Which of us is speaking here? I try to catch my breath, feel my heart flutter, feel myself freezing from the feet up. I'm aware of Lamont awakening, turning his head, looking up at me as if aroused by some silent signal; he groans, much the same sound as he made a few weeks ago at the shelter when he heard me say I couldn't take him home with me.

Thuy has leaned across the coffee table. She is almost, but not quite, touching my hand. "Are you all right, Mr. Keyshot? Are you all right?" Her tone is anxious. Her expression is concerned.

She leaves her chair and kneels at my side, searches my face. "Don't cry, Mr. Keyshot." She raises a hand as if to brush the tear from my cheek, but she does not touch. "It's not so bad. I'm not gonna die right away, I think. I dit'n mean to make you cry. I dit'n think *that* would happen. I dit'n mean for that to happen."

"Sorry, Thuy. Your story just brought up some things from my own life, is all. Surprised me and I couldn't hold it in, I guess."

"You're dying, too. Ah! Yes, you always did look like it."

That additional piece of unsolicited criticism sobers me quickly. "Well, we're *all* dying, aren't we, Thuy; it's just that some of us are going more quickly than we'd anticipated." I didn't mean to let that out, but she takes it in stride, moves back to her chair, seems to relax into it.

"Hey, you talk straight. I think my father would have talked straight like that. It's not true what Richie Kuhl said about you. I'm glad I came up here, Mr. Keyshot."

"Hey, I'm glad you did, too."

"Can I come again?"

"I'll expect you to. Would you care for some cocoa?"

"Sounds good."

We have cocoa and she talks on for another 15 minutes about the weather, teachers she liked and didn't like, differences among famous violinists, international geography, and favorite foods. I watch and admire and respond occasionally. This, I decide, is a 17-year-old going on 70 who sings the tunes with her own words—and may never stop at all.

Perhaps I have made a friend. I surely have a new client. I hope I can help.

Chapter Twenty

I am feeling cheerful, totally cheerful, moreso than I've felt for many months—perhaps for years. Even the twice-weekly sessions with Junior and Bobby R. have not seemed burdensome. I have had no bad dreams, no flashbacks, no headaches, no great pains. I am looking forward to the holiday season, especially to the choral concert series that Nim Chaud plans to bring to Tabernacle from the Delta University Conservatory. Even the incessant Christmas music that bores its twanging through the floor from Mr. D.H. Carp's Groceries & Sundries does not especially bother me. It is good to be alive. Was it Mother Crinkle's whacks on my head that produced all this blessing?

Thuy has not called or returned, nor has Ms Penny Preene, but that's probably the native reticence of those women, each different but essentially similar: not feeling their troubles are worth bothering someone else with. They will each overcome that, I'm sure; with my guidance, I hope.

No more word from Mitzi, whose San Francisco gig obviously did not turn out, but whose application to a Fresno radio station evidently produced at least a trial as commentator on national politics, women's affairs, and health and hygiene. Her skill with the Spanish language has helped her there, and the management has modified her on-air name to Miriam Chiflada.

I have my clock radio set to the station so each morning Lamont and I awaken to Mitzi's honeyed tones, sometimes speaking Spanish. The hair on the back of Lamont's neck stands up when he hears her voice, and he glances questioningly at me. I only smile. Our Seventh Avenue *menage à cinq* is history.

Joseph Kuhl has dropped in several times. Joseph is not one who feels his troubles are bothersome to others. But his most recent visit was not about troubles, per se.

"Well, I guess I deserve a bonus, wut'n you say, Mr. Keyshot?

"How's that, Joseph? Why a bonus?"

"Well, fooey! Don't you know? I helped you starting in to think detectively. You know. What I mean is, this don't, dut'n happen by accident. I was mentoring you, y'know? And now lookit how it come out! You got Whatisname—Lamont—back, and you figured out who whacked you on the head, and you know who sent you that dumb pasted-up note—hey, you thought I dit'n know about that?—and you probably got a whole bunch of new looneys to help out, and what's even better—something my dad thinks is the smartest thing you ever done, you got your wife off of your back. My dad is always wishing he could get his wife off of his back. 'Course he's never ast me for my advice about that." Joe shows his teeth. A nice smile, totally unconstipated, winning friends and influencing people.

"Well, I appreciate that. Of course, I thought I recalled all along that your mentoring me was all part of the originally agreed-upon service. Am I in error about that? Am I mis-remembering?"

"Oh. Well."

Joe looks so profoundly disappointed, his head hanging, his eyebrows almost joined in pain, that I nearly...but I decide not to be victimized for a change. "But I'll be sure to consider recommending you for similar work, should anyone ask."

"Oh, well. What I mean is, never hurts to ast, right?"

Joseph leaves, whistling "Go Baloney" down the stairs. He has the thing with feathers by the tail.

The surprise of the month—or perhaps the year—is my new client, assigned by Chaud County, an indigent who presents with indications of amnesia according to the client himself. Actually, were this client an amnesiac, he would be treated in-house at the county hospital by a team of psychiatrists, social workers, et al. I have learned that several lawyers are beseeching this fellow to be their client, for it is allegedly the tragic fall from his hospital bed that has left him bereft of memory—a fall precipitated by incompetent and uncaring physicians, nurses, technicians, and clerks.

The sheriff's representative, however, tells me a slightly different story. The fellow was apprehended with cash and other valuables allegedly pilfered from fellow patients in Doctors Hospital where said client was recovering from several blows to the head, minor injuries according to the file.

My new client is Jess Pleroma. Or perhaps it is again Wolfgang von Pleroma. He is due at any moment now.

"Hey, guy!" The head pops through the un-knocked doorway. It is curly and partly bearded. The eyes are brown, sharp, and bright. The teeth are white, sharp. The Cheshire smile increases as I turn from my sink.

"C'mon in. Have a seat." I wave him to the client's chair, but he wanders around the room examining my library, my music collection, my small sculptures and framed prints, my view of Front Street. I wipe my hands on a dish towel and pour us both a cup of tea. "You drink tea?"

"Hey, yeh. I drink anything free. Heh-heh."

He tousels Lamont's head. Lamont only smiles. Interesting.

We are seated, facing. I begin. "You are...?" The question is designed to elicit the autobiography and clues as to the problem as seen by the client.

"Yeh." This one word constitutes the response. Then the coda. "Tea is weird. No bag."

"Made with the leaves, y'know. You steep the leaves in the pot."

"Oh. Yeh. Steep the leaves. Well. Still weird." He sets the cup on the carpet next to his chair, instead of on the table in front of him.

"I believe you're Jess Pleroma."

"Yeh. Well, maybe. I don't, y'know, actually know who I am because of this, like, y'know, big accident I had where I not only got, y'know, whacked on the head by that old lady, I sort of fell down in the hospital and hit my head there, too."

"You're not bandaged."

"Well, the dumb doctors over there cut'n find, y'know, any wound. I told 'em it was, y'know, like a subdural hemitoma, but they said, 'yeh, yeh, we know,' and dit'n do anything about it."

He uses *subdural* like a medical pro.

"Lotta bullshit. Well, I'll get a piece of 'em." He squints his eyes and shows his teeth, picks up his cup and sips. "Not so bad when you, like, y'know, get used to it."

"You were Wolfgang von Pleroma a couple weeks ago."

"Oh, yeh? Was I? Well, I'm a, y'know, creative type of a guy." He puts his cup on the table this time, now looks me in the eye. "And I know who you are, too. Since I slept in your bed." He smiles this time with his lips closed. He's as sneaky as he looks. There, there, Don. Put away the prejudices.

"I heard. I hope Ab didn't disturb your slumber."

"Who? Oh, the old dude in the picture. Yeh! Got a good, y'know, hard look on him."

"Nim Chaud tells me you're 'Brother Browne'."

"Brother Browne. Oh, yeh. Brother Browne. Well, that's when I'm in my Bible mood, like." He smirks.

"So, for the record or maybe, first, off the record, who are you, actually?"

"Who am I actually? Well, now that I'm sort of, like, recovering pieces of my memory, I'm Judge Ordway's grandson, first of all." He looks closely at me. Do I believe him? "Maybe a nephew?"

"Bellona Shaw says you're Judge Ordway's son Mark's, ah, dead wife Elaine's, um, step-brother."

"Oh, well. That, too, maybe." He puts down his cup, again on the table. Looks pained. "I don't really know who I am. Does anybody?"

This hits home. Don Keyshot has been searching for himself all his life. Has he found himself yet? "Yes, *does* anybody? Does Mark Ordway?"

"Oh, Mark. He knows who he is. And Jack. He knows. And Tery, his little sister. She knows. Yeh, they all know who they are. But like Kirkegaard says, *know thyself.* So I'm, like, trying to know myself. Gotta find myself first, maybe?"

I don't criticize his choice of philosopher. "Elvis Drumhandler has told me that you are actually Doctor Jess Schweitzer-Ordway, a physician and his artistic advisor."

"Elvis's, like, a creative person, too, y'know."

"And last summer you were Leonardo diPleroma."

"Yeh, well, that was, like, in my Hollywood producer days, y'know."

"So, you're well aware that these personae are fictitious."

"What?"

"You know you're putting people on."

"Oh. Hell, yes! You think I'm crazy?"

"I can't discern any any mental disease from here."

He looks at me closely, his head forward, his arms flat on the arms of the chair. "There's a difference? I never found anybody, y'know, who *cared* whether I was telling the truth. In fact, most people would, like, better hear a story, y'know? It *amuses* 'em. And *amused* people are, like, y'know, more likely to pay up. Got it?"

"I think so."

"Kinda like your missus."

"Ah. Ex-missus."

"Whatever. She was looking for kicks." Maybe Jess believes I want to hear about Mitzi and him.

"Well, whatever you and my ex-wife got up to is not relevant here, is it?"

"It'n it? Okay, I can just say, like, buddy, I know what you had to put up with. Jeezus, that old bag is something else. No, I don't mean Mitzi—I cut'n put up with her, either. But, no, I mean the old lady, the one konked me. And the dyke always hanging around. Man, no wonder you moved out." He looks about the room again, an admiring sweep this time. "I wut'n mind staying here, y'know? You maybe looking for a room-mate?"

"I have one." I indicate Lamont who smacks his lips and turns over.

"Well, anyways, you gonna cure me of my evil nature?"

"Is that your problem?"

"Hey, you tell me! Mitzi got away with her green Jag. Hey, now there's a fukup for you, a problem, like? I thought for sure I was, like, gonna get that baby. I was all set to tool the Giant down the Interstate to Los Angeles, drag the main down there in Hollywood, y'know?" He wags his head sadly. "She was gone before I could, y'know, take the distributor cap off and make like I needed to fix it. You know that game. Shee-it. The old lady took care of that with her cane. Never even seen *that* coming. And when I got out of the hospital and come back here for my tennis racket and golf clubs, my bags was on the porch and Mitzi was packed and gone. Some women don't have no artistic feeling." Jess scratches his jaw, his underarms, his crotch. "I just got chickled that time, I guess" He smirks. "That's what the Kuhls say when they think they been, y'know, screwed. *Chickled.*"

"What's going to become of you, Jess? Have you any ambitions, strengths?"

"I'm gonna live fast and have a good time. Anything wrong with that? And I got a lot of hope for my future."

"You've spent a lot of time in jail. Anything wrong with that?"

"That's because people got no, like, y'know, sense of humor. The sheriff's got no sense of humor."

"How do you think I can help you?"

"You help me, like cure me? Hey, no offense, guy, but, y'know, you gotta maybe cure yourself first, right? But as long as the county's paying, I'll be glad to, y'know, come back and, like, drink your tea, help you along. Maybe next time you ought to offer a guy something to eat, y'know?"

I try to show no reaction, only smile tolerantly, open my appointment book, suggest a date and time for another meeting.

He smiles broadly, agrees. "I made a couple points in psychology there, did I? No offense. You can call me Sigmund." He reaches across the table to shake my hand. How can I refuse to respond to such a charming gesture? Hope. He says he has a lot of hope. Jess Pleroma reaches down and scratches Lamont's ears again. Lamont smiles. Jess has won Lamont as a friend, and influenced him. As Jess leaves I erase "Jess" from my appointment book and write in "Sigmund." Who knows, maybe he will be helpful.

❦
Chapter Twenty-one

My next visitor is a real surprise, a man I had considered to be a friend throughout my time at Balona High—until the end of my teaching career, when occurred that "firing" phenomenon that still puzzles me. I hadn't seen him, except at a distance, since my last day at Balona High.

He knocks at my office door without the usual clamor people make on the stairs. "Anybody in there? You in there?"

"Come in, Abel." I recognize Principal Abel Croon's voice at once, my having that kind of memory and his having that unusually memorable kind of trumpeting tenor voice, a *command voice.* One of my sergeants had a voice like that. Abel even looks like the sergeant, same small close-set pale blue eyes, except Abel is soft-looking, not fit. We shake hands and he takes a seat in my client chair without invitation and with a great sigh. His head and neck are bright red, perhaps from the exertion of stair-climbing, exercise not being something he enjoys or is known to seek. When he happens to glance down and see Lamont in his pillow box, Abel rises up quickly to his full five-seven and backs away.

"Does it bite?"

"No, he's a very friendly animal." Abel is almost ready to kick at Lamont's pillow box. Even calm as he is, Lamont would take exception to that, I'm sure. "You should just have a seat and relax."

"I think maybe I'm allergic to dogs. They tend to bite me." This is certainly true, as even Manon, Miss

Candy Wishingfor's dog—a youngster who when not participating in sexual activity on First Avenue or in the quad spends her days under Miss Candy's desk gazing out between Miss Candy's elegant ankles—even Manon tends to growl when Abel passes by. Of course, there is no such rude behavior from Lamont who feels keenly his position as co-host of this place.

"Lamont won't bite you. Guaranteed. So, what brings you here, Abel? Did I win the Big Baloney raffle and you're here to pay off?" Abel exercises his professional grimace, first at my use of the disgraceful nickname for his school, and second at my mentioning the illegal and very profitable gambling venture that aids the football, wrestling, and basketball programs at the school. He sinks back into the chair, casting a suspicious glance at Lamont and easing his body so that he's sitting on the farther side.

"I came up here to mend fence. Sort of." He reaches for a tissue from my box and blows his nose, wipes his head, looks for a receptacle, evidently doesn't see the basket behind his elbow, drops the tissue on the floor near Lamont. "People at Solidarity keep harping that you got some kind of a raw deal. So I been having to try to mend my own fence over there all summer and fall." *Solidarity* is the business fellowship organization to which belong most Balona males who don't work with their hands. The club meets for breakfast in Delta City every week. I was once a regular and am now an occasional.

"I have put it out of my mind, Abel. I understand how pressed you were financially. If I had been principal, I might have made the same choice." I would *not* have made the same choice, and we both know it, but I have no alternatives to propose.

"Well, I'm not talking about that." He shrugs his shoulders, jitters in the chair, taps his fingers on the arms, looks at the ceiling. "I mean the rumor about

Turkey Dwindle and all that. You know." He reaches for another tissue, wipes his horn-rim glasses, again tosses the tissue to the carpet.

"Ah. Well, Abel, I know about the rumor now. I didn't then. Somebody might have told me what the charges were. Might have gone down a little differently if I'd known at the time what Sammy Joe was talking about when he said I 'liked some kids real good.'"

"Oh, there wat'n *charges*, for heavensakes." Abel's tone is somewhat peevish. "Mr. Sam Joe Sly was just repeating stuff he'd heard around, probably made up by Sammy Jack. Sammy Jack is Mr. Sam Joe Sly's kid, y'know. *Charges*. You make it sound so, so formal like."

"Formal enough, Abel. Formal enough to get rid of me."

I notice that Abel hasn't once used my name during our dialog. I'm trying to think back in our various after-school conversations if he's ever used my name in the friendly bantering way of comrades. It's interesting if not necessarily useful or helpful to evaluate one's relationships occasionally, especially at some distance. I had considered Abel Croon to be a friend.

"So, anyways, Amy Dwindle brought her kid Turkey...prob'ly I should ought to quit calling the kid that. Anyways, she brought Dirk into the office a couple months ago."

"You appear to have assumed the counselor's role."

"Yeh, dammit. Driving me crazy. Just the paperwork's enough to drive me looney. Anyways, Amy Dwindle said she heard the rumor about you and Dirk from Sophie at Kute Kurls & Nails, too, so she went and chewed out Turkey, made sure there wat'n anything to confess. So she came to see me and made him tell me to my face. Why me, I don't know. Shut've gone to see Mr. Sam Joe Sly, actually. Told him instead."

"So, Abel, why are you here?"

"Well, I wanted to let you know there was no hard feelings."

"I never had hard feelings, Abel. Oh, I was mildly depressed for three or four months, had a few hate-calls and Mitzi considered disconnecting the phone. My marriage collapsed. I had headaches and other pains. I hadn't yet received my final counseling license and was concerned about that. My dog disappeared. I was whacked on the head and ended up in the hospital, and it was a while before my retirement pay came through—but other than those minor things, I was just fine." Perhaps I have laid it on a bit thick. Abel Croon is now sweating again. I rise and consult the thermostat: 68 degrees. I turn it down a bit, always feeling quite comfortable in cool rooms, especially as I'm wearing, as usual, sweat clothing and heavy wool socks. "And I'm glad you harbor no hard feelings."

"Well, there was something else."

"Something besides the report from a few months ago about the conference you had with Dirk Dwindle and his mother?"

"You make it sound like I was keeping it back on purpose." Abel's tone whines, much like quasi-French teacher Sid Weiner complaining about always being cheated by Balonans. "You got to realize what a big job it is over there being principal. I got all kinds of stuff on my mind and duties to perform and can't go around making trips all the time just to patch up hard feelings, eksedra."

"Was the *something else* perhaps about Beauty Jean Dwindle?"

"Oh. I almost forgot about that one." Abel smiles. Should I tell him at last that he needs to visit his dentist? "Yeh. That wat'n what I came over here about, but it's funny, so I'll pass it along. About Beauty Jean—what a name!—about Beauty Jean: Now she's in love with Sheriff Anson Chaud, of all people. Says he's a champion of the little people, gonna work for his re-election campaign, carries his picture in a locket around her neck. Comes in every day to tell me about it, and cry."

"About the reason you're here, Abel."

"Oh, yeh, that. Well, another reason I'm here is that the guys in Solidarity say I should tell you to come on back regular. I should say guys and *gals*, since you might have noticed we got a dozen women members in now, all gabbling at once. Breakfast sounds like a chicken house. Can't hardly hear yourself eating, y'know." He heaves a sigh, as if unburdening himself of a heavy load. "So that's it."

His chest and shoulders are still tight; he's got something else on his mind.

"I'll give it some thought, Abel, but it all depends on how busy I get. My practice is growing." I smile without meaning to appear self-satisfied, but that's probably the way Abel sees the smile.

"Well, actually, the reason I'm here it'n all about what I said so far. I mean about Turkey and Bootsie and Solidarity. That stuff."

"You have another reason."

"Well, the real actual reason is, my new board member is all hot to spend some money we don't have on a part-time counselor. Got the other four members stirred up, y'know. So they're now saying maybe you'd be interested in coming back part-time, since it's legal that way to retire you and still pay you." Abel wipes his head again. "I had to tell 'em that, y'know. So that's actually why I'm here." He sits looking at me, reddish eyebrows up over his eyeglass frames. "Well? It'd get me off of the hook."

Abel Croon is asking me to get him "off the hook." He hasn't mentioned the name of the new school board member, Mark Ordway, a man I respect and admire. How should I handle this? Make them beg?

"I'll give it some thought, but it all depends on how busy I get. My practice is growing."

He frowns, perhaps recognizing my phrasing from an earlier response. "You mean you're not all that eager to come back, even if it's only for part time? I wut've thought you'd jump at the chance to make an extra buck or two—and show Balona the charges were not true."

"What charges?" I squint my eyes as if pondering. "I'll give it some thought." I reach down and scratch Lamont's head. Lamont yawns, notices Abel Croon, frowns, goes back to sleep. Perhaps Lamont is telling me something. I try to engage Abel in pleasant conversation, practice some social skills Mitzi always accused me of lacking. "I've always wondered, Abel, where did you get your training to be a high school principal?"

"Training? What training? I was a guy brought in. Y'know, *brought in*, where somebody takes a look at the great job you're doing in the classroom and tells you, 'Come on in and be a vice-principal, and then we'll promote you when you show you can do the job.' That's what *brought in* means. When you get brought in, you get your board to certify that you're necessary, and then every once in a while you take a dumb course or two to satisfy the State. That's all. That was over in Delta City. It's probably different now. Was I *trained?*

"No way. I watched old Lucy and that dumb Kork and saw what they did wrong, decided not to do those things. Maybe that's training. But you either got it or you don't. I'm one of those guys who's got it."

I suddenly see light leaking from a closet. Not a real closet. A metaphorical closet. "Why are you really here, Abel?"

He looks into my eyes for 20 seconds, saying not a word.

The eyes are brimming. "Since you left I don't have anybody to talk with."

Not feeling all that charitable at the moment, I put it on a purely professional basis. "We could fix that, Abel. You could come on up here every week for an hour and we could talk. Or you could even come twice a week when you were feeling particular pressures."

"Oh. You mean like come up here and seek professional help?"

"Exactly. Seek professional help."

"Well. I don't know about that. If you was to come back part time we could probably talk a lot more, I would think, right there in the office."

"But then we'd have our talks interrupted by youngsters and parents and Doctor Thrust and Miss Candy—the way our talks used to be interrupted. Remember?"

"Yeh. Well, I'll give it some thought. And you'll give it some thought, too, okay, Don, and let me know right soon?"

We left it at that and Abel Croon left. I sat and had a cup of tea and thought about how Sergeant Breene, nervous and impatient, must have had his own private demons, and how perhaps it was a pity we never got to know the real man.

⚜ Chapter Twenty-two

In three days time, Ms Penny Preene calls. "I'm calling about Thuy."

"Delightful young woman. Thanks so much for directing her my way. We had a good visit and she thinks she'll come back."

"Oh. No, she won't be able to, Mr. Keyshot. Thuy passed over last night." In Balona, *passed over* means died.

I don't know how to respond except to say, after the 10 seconds in which my heart has stopped and I can't breathe, "I'm sorry." There's the taste of iron in my mouth. I put the phone down without doing the appropriate sign-offs. I feel the way I felt in-country when I heard somebody was lost in combat: the report was unreal. No, it must be true, they're packing up his gear. In my mind, I could see the man's smiling and frowning face, bearded and clean-shaven, hear his laugh, reconstruct the sound of his joke-telling and cursing and complaining, but I would never see him again.

I was sad. I was also ashamed for being glad that this time, at least, I was not the one in the bag.

But I'm not glad this time.

Penny Preene's call swept me back in time to that experience when I was about to finish boot camp at Parris Island. A runner had come to the barracks late at night with a message from battalion: *Report to the commanding officer.* I reported, wondering what I had done wrong.

The exec told me to sit. I sat. He pulled up a chair next to me, knee to knee, told me the news. There had been an accident and I was needed at home. Did I have any relatives other than my immediate family? No. Should I call my mom first before I go home? I asked.

No, was the reply. You need now to be more of what you've been learning to be: a United States Marine. You need now to brace-to and maintain-an-even-strain, take what comes like the man you are. Your parents are dead, Son.

I did my best to brace-to and maintain-an-even-strain, taking the bus from camp and wondering all the way to New Jersey what I would find when I got there.

I discovered that I was in charge of the squad, that my parents and my little brother and little sister had all bought it on the Turnpike, my dad driving. Apparently he and my mother had both been celebrating another holiday. It was a strange experience with four coffins in the church, and priests suggesting that I find solace in prayer and that I also try to find ways to reimburse the church for their financial outlay as the church was having a hard time.

There had been no insurance. The local government saw to the disposition of my family's property, such as had not already in life been pawned or sold. My legacy was my Comfortable Dream and seven photographs. I managed to brace-to and maintain-an-even-strain and was in Vietnam within six weeks.

Thinking about loss and change, about Thuy's bravery, and about maintaining an even strain, I crawled into my cot and under my blanket. I wept. Lamont crept onto the cot and lay on my legs, comforting. We stayed there for a while, until I decided to get on with it. Perhaps maintaining an even strain is more productive.

I explained my situation to Nim Chaud, believing that he might accompany me to visit Thuy's family. Why I thought such a visit would appeal to him I don't know. He didn't know the young woman or her family. But Nim has a presence that people find comforting. My presence could hardly be of comfort, could it?

"Perhaps you could think farther into that—as to whether or not your visiting might bring some comfort to the family.

"She never came in for counseling at Balona High."

"It's said that many refugees of Asian origin believe their woes are nobody's business, and that it's not polite to complain. They do have a point, don't they!"

Of course I walked alone under dark clouds to Thuy's home. The women had set up a small altar in the living room. Candles, images, incense. A young Buddhist monk sat there in his saffron robe and sandals drinking tea and reading a newspaper. I had brought a bag of tangerines, not knowing what else to bring that might be more appropriate. At Nim's suggestion I selected fruit with leaves. I said to the mother that I thought Thuy was a wonderful girl and I liked her and wished I'd come to know her better.

The tiny mother, smaller and even more pale than her daughter, was wearing a white headband. She took the fruit, nodded and looked straight ahead and smiled a thin smile, perhaps understanding, if not the words, then the obvious sentiment.

"You Mister Don? You marine, Vietnam?" The mother looked into my eyes. I nodded. "I'm sorry," she said. "You wait." I waited while she left the room and returned bearing a white envelope. "From Trinh. Thuy. For you." I took the envelope, bowed my head to her and pressed my palms together in the gesture I had seen over there so many times, and she nodded and bowed to me and went to the door, opened it, and stood there, head lowered.

So I left the house and stood on the porch for a few minutes, waiting for the rain to stop, wishing I had worn my rainhat.

The door opened and the mother handed me a black umbrella. "Not get sick," she said and closed the door once again. I trudged off home in the rain, but fairly dry because of the mother's thoughtfulness.

The note from Thuy was handwritten in blue ink. Probably a fountain pen rather than a ballpoint for the words had made no impression into the paper. "For Mr. Don Keyshot" was written on the envelope.

> *Dear Mr. Keyshot, I was afraid you might not hear what I was saying, but I think you did. I never told anyone those things I said. Not even my best aunty. But I was able to say them to you. I wish I had come to see you before. If I feel better I will see you again and I will tell you this. If I don't feel better, you will get this note. The thing I want to remember is that every time I feel good, it is a cause to celebrate and hope for the best. Same for every time I have made somebody else feel good or have thought good thoughts. You helped me think good thoughts and also feel good. I feel that probably we will meet again, somehow. Your student,*
>
> *Thuy Le*

It is difficult to hold this note while my hands shake so. I can only hope that Thuy and I will meet again, somehow.

Life is painful.

❦
Chapter Twenty-three

"I saw the little girl coming out of here, y'know, a while back. Pretty little thing. Sad looking, though. Sad, was she?" Bellona is quizzing me again about my clients, this time about Thuy, of course. Probably she can view my doorway from her office window at the *Courier*. Still, it must be a stretch as the paper is across Front Street down the block a good 75 meters. Bellona's desk must be at the corner of the building so she can keep her eye on Front Street happenings.

"Bellona, I can't discuss my clients."

"She's departed though. Can't you discuss your departed clients? I mean, who's to know?"

"Probably all of Balona, don't you think?"

"Well, that's not a nice thing to say to a journalist with tight lips." She has seated herself on my cot instead of in the client's chair. I am seated in the therapist's chair. She raises her head. "See how tight my lips are?" Bellona has pretty lips, and not heavily made-up.

"I can see that, Bellona. But the thing stands."

"Have you heard the news about Penny Preene and Mark Ordway? That they're getting married? Finally? About time! I'm writing it up. Why don't you come over here and sit. See close-up how tight my lips are. Or aren't. It's a lot more comfortable here."

It couldn't be more comfortable there, as the cot is a war-surplus barracks model and the mattress is nothing but a thin foam pad through which every morning I can trace the marks of the springs on my flesh.

The pad is so thin I have been considering replacing it with a genuine tick. "It's actually a lot more comfortable right here, where I can see you without destroying my neck and re-opening my headwounds."

"Maybe so. I'll try it." She rises, crosses the space quickly, and deposits herself on my lap. "You romantic devil! You can't help flirting with a girl, can you!"

I didn't realize I was flirting, but she is not very heavy and she smells good. Peppermint, probably. I lock my hands across my chest, fasten my gaze on Lamont who is watching this spectacle from his pillow-box. He has raised his head so he won't miss anything.

"I have wanted to give you a little kiss for ever so long."

"Well, I don't know." I lick my lips in anticipation. This is ridiculous and distinctly unprofessional, but sort of nice.

"Well, if you don't know, then I don't know." Bellona rises at once and sits in the client chair, looks steadily at the carpet, turns dark red. "I'm sorry. I thought you might like to give me a kiss. Sort of make sure we're friends, like. Well, law, a girl can make a mistake." Finally she looks up. "I guess I made a mistake?"

"I'm sorry. I'm just so surprised. Taken unawares, y'know."

"You want me to leave?"

"How come? Why should I want that?"

"Well, I've made a fool of myself."

"I'd say you've expressed yourself very effectively. It's I who should apologize for being such a fogey. So, I apologize for being such a fogey."

I am feeling uncomfortable, nevertheless. "But I have to tell you, I have some mixed emotions here, y'know. You're my client and I have to maintain a certain professional distance from my clients or I can't do my job properly. Same as you when you're investigating for a story. You can't get too close to your subject or your perspective gets warped. Isn't that true?"

She is smiling.

"You said you have mixed emotions."

"Yes. Mixed. Well, I do also find you attractive, y'know."

"Ah! Ah! Well, now we're getting some place. You could call me 'Bell.' It's what my best friends called me when I was a girl. Bell." She frowns. "I don't want you to get the wrong idear. I don't go around making up to any old man. I mean any man; I dit'n mean the *old*."

"Do you want to finish your interview?"

"What interview's that?"

"Your interview of Mr. Don Crinkle." I smile now, putting us both at ease. Oops, I should not have smiled; we are not both at ease.

"This is more personal, Don, and has nothing to do with that interview thing, and Mitzi Crinkle is the last person I want to talk about right now. So don't change the subject on me. I mean, please. What I would like to say is, I find you a most attractive man, even though you are sort of slippery, and I would like to see you more often. Not on a professional basis. On a personal basis. Maybe with the thought of some kind of long-term relationship in mind, y'know?"

"I see."

"You 'see.' Does that mean you might be interested, too?"

"Sure. Interested, sure. It's just that there are some things I would have to explain. There would be some necessary limits to that relationship."

"Well, I'm not all that eager to jump into bed—or a marriage, either!"

"No, I meant other considerations."

"Ah. Well, I have some limitations, too, if you could remember some of the things I told you about my relationship. About my, my marriage, such as it was."

"Yes. I remember."

"I like hugging and kissing—not that I do that sort of thing, of course; I don't hug-and-kiss-around, you know, but as for the other thing, I don't much like it, not that I've had much experience at it, y'know. But you went and volunteered the information that you're a highly moral man and you don't like to do the other thing, either. So maybe we got something going here?"

Bellona hadn't listened to my "moral" explanation. She was busy hearing her own interpretation, a common problem in counseling.

I'll put off explanations until perhaps we know each other better. Isn't that what Nim Chaud would do?

No, Nim would probably face it straight on, and salt the argument with sentiments about creative loving, et cetera. I'm not ready to present the issues to Bellona.

It didn't work with Mitzi because Mitzi was interested in other modes.

It might work with Bellona, if I come to appreciate Bellona the way she appears ready to appreciate me.

"It's nice to be appreciated. I'm glad you like Lamont. And Lamont likes you, too."

Lamont closes his eyes, smiles.

"Let me tell you about my happy childhood, Don. By the way, just because we have a relationship going here doesn't mean I won't pay you for your counseling services, hear? And I intend to use all my contacts to help you build your practice, hear?"

"Oh, good. I hear that, Bell."

I brew us some black tea and start up a CD and we drink tea with a background of Henry Mancini oldies. and Bell begins to tell me about her happy childhood.

There is hope, the thing with feathers that perches in the soul. It is good to be alive. Ω

South Lake Tahoe, California

About the Author

When teacher-author Jonathan Pearce is not telling tales for Balona Books or teaching a class or mowing the lawn or doing chores around the house, or responding to welcome e-mail (Jonathan@Balona.com) about his stories, he is probably reading a good book or practicing, in sweaty enthusiasm, one of several Asian martial arts.

He also plays the cello, is obedient to his wife and cat, loves his family, and writes daily.

He has indeed humped the boonies, in a military manner, in a war.

BalonaBooks ®
http://www.balona.com